Untamed

Untamed

JoAnn Ross

WHEELER
CHIVERS

This Large Print edition is published by Wheeler Publishing, Waterville, Maine USA and by BBC Audiobooks, Ltd, Bath, England.

Published in 2005 in the U.S. by arrangement with Harlequin Books S.A.

Published in 2005 in the U.K. by arrangement with Harlequin Enterprises II, B.V.

U.S. Hardcover 1-58724-812-3 (Romance)
U.K. Hardcover 1-4056-3316-6 (Chivers Large Print)
U.K. Softcover 1-4056-3317-4 (Camden Large Print)

The text of this Large Print edition is unabridged.
Other aspects of the book may vary from the original edition.

Set in 16 pt. Plantin by Ramona Watson.

Printed in the United States on permanent paper.

British Library Cataloguing-in-Publication Data available

Library of Congress Cataloging-in-Publication Data

Ross, JoAnn.
      Untamed / JoAnn Ross.
         p. cm.
      ISBN 1-58724-812-3 (lg. print : hc : alk. paper)
      1. Secrecy — Fiction.   2. Large type books.   I. Title.
   PS3568.O843485U57 2005
                                                    2004057248

Untamed

1

A full moon rode high in the mid-night sky, casting a shimmering silver light over the ancient forest, il-luminating the lone woman who moved with the suppleness of a sleek jungle panther amidst the tangled trunks of the leafless oak trees. Her hooded black cape blended into the shadows as she made her way through the swirling mists of fog to the clearing.

The night was silent save for the sad sigh of the north wind in the tops of the towering pine trees, the occasional sweet, lonely cry of an owl, the croaks of frogs in the meadow pond. The familiar night sounds were primal music to the woman's ears, reaching deep into her soul, stirring the wildness that lurked in her heart.

It was music from an ancient time, a time when primitive man trembled with fear against the unseen denizens of the dark night. A time when her people ruled with wisdom and power.

A time of magic.

When she reached the clearing, the woman turned her exquisite face skyward and received a warm infusion of energy from her mother, the moon. She lifted her arms, palms turned upward toward the icy stars. Her ripe vermilion lips began chanting words taught to her while still in her cradle. Words passed down from generation to generation, words that flowed warmly through her veins along with the blood that made her who she was.

And what she was.

A witch.

Her greeting completed, she slipped off the hooded cape and let it fall to the ground. The wind caught her freed long hair, whipping it into a wild jet froth about her face. Beneath the hood, she was wearing the clothes she always donned when fighting those who would use the night to cloak their evil ways.

The jet metal breastplate of the sleek black bodysuit shaped her lush breasts into two glistening cones in a way that was designed to send male pulses hammering. Black leather boots encased her long legs to mid-thigh.

Around her neck, she wore a silver chain on which hung a silver amulet that nestled between those glorious, uplifted breasts. The woman opened the amulet and took out a small vial of scented oil, which she sprinkled over the wood she'd already gathered and stacked in the sacred circle of stones.

With the powers of midnight vibrating through her, she held her hands out over the wood, which instantly ignited in a whoosh of wind and flame.

Closing her eyes, feeling the heat of the crackling fire in the marrow of her bones, the woman known as Morganna concentrated on the faces of her enemies. In her mind she saw them melting like candles amidst the dancing, deadly flames. She heard their agonized screams. And suf-

fered their pain. Spellmakers who dealt in the dark side did not escape unscathed.

A lethal heat suffused her, fire flicked at her nerve endings, but Morganna did not flinch. Nor did she cry out. These acts of vengeance were her calling. Since her fate was both preordained and inescapable, she bore her pain in silence.

And when it was completed, when the scorching flames gave way to the cooling, comforting rain, she lifted her arms once again to the midnight sky and offered a prayer of thanksgiving.

"It is done," she said finally, breathing a deep, satisfied sigh of achievement.

She was physically and psychically drained. Her legs had as much substance as the sea as she slowly folded to the ground. For an unfathomable time her mind was washed clean, healing her of the torturous burdens she'd willingly undertaken.

"It is done."
Gavin Thomas nodded with satisfaction

as he signed his name to the last frame of this latest adventure of Morganna, Mistress of the Night.

The crime-fighting witch had outdone herself this time. And looked damn good while doing it, he decided, casting a judicial eye over the full-color drawing of the luscious female body glowing orange and silver from the moon and firelight.

Gavin would be the first to admit that his creation probably stirred up the hormonal juices in more than one teenage male. But what was so wrong with that? he'd asked detractors on more than one occasion. Besides, his graphic novels — which those same detractors insisted on calling comic books — were not nearly as sexually explicit as the stuff kids saw every day on those rock and rap videos on MTV.

And Morganna, while admittedly dabbling in black magic, was, after all, a force for good. For truth, justice, Mom, apple pie and the American way.

She was, he'd told late-night TV talk-show host Tom Snyder just last week, this generation's Superman. But a lot better looking.

He'd even finished up the interview by saying that if he ever met a female who was half the woman the fictitious Morganna

11

was, he'd marry her on the spot.

Tom had laughed — that familiar too-many-cigarettes rasp — as he was supposed to. What the talk-show host had no way of knowing was that Gavin wasn't joking.

The letter arrived in the morning mail. Tara Delaney did not have to open the cream linen envelope to know what the letter inside would say. The return address — from an Arizona attorney — told her all she needed to know.

Why wouldn't they leave her alone?

She tossed the letter unopened into the wastebasket beside her desk, went into her bedroom and tried to resume packing for her long overdue vacation. With her usual attention to detail, she'd planned the trip to Kauai months ago. A beachfront condo was booked for the next two weeks, her airline tickets had been purchased weeks ago and she'd even bought two new bikinis and a sheer white cover-up. Tomorrow she'd be lying on the beach, soaking up the tropical sun and beginning to make her way through the stack of novels she was always buying but never had time to read.

"You deserve this vacation," she reminded herself as she packed her toiletries.

"You've earned it." She tossed the sun-block into a plastic-lined zipper bag. "You can't let anything — or anyone — stand in your way."

It was a dandy little pep talk, and it should have worked. Would have worked had it not been for the siren call of that discarded letter.

"Oh, hell." She stomped back into the living room, pulled the envelope out of the wastebasket and opened it with the sterling-silver opener fashioned in the shape of a Celtic cross she'd received as a Midsummer Day gift from her artist father. The paragraph of legalese repeated what the other letters had told her: that she was now the proud owner of a one-hundred-year-old Victorian house in Whiskey River, Arizona.

Sighing, she put the letter down, picked up the phone and dialed a number she knew by heart.

"Hello, Tara dear," the smoothly modulated voice answered after the first ring. "I was just thinking of you."

Tara stifled a sigh. "It figures."

"A mother always knows when her child is upset," Lina Delaney said. "As you'll discover yourself someday."

Tara was suddenly reminded of all the

times while she was growing up she'd tried to put something over on her mother. And failed.

"It would be nice," she said crankily, "if just once I could keep something to myself."

"Your thoughts are your own, Tara." Her mother's tone remained steadfastly calm, as always. "I would certainly never pry."

Tara decided this was not the time to mention that little episode during her seventeenth summer when she'd lied about a slumber party at Mary Bretton's house in order to spend the night with Jeff Townsend, whose parents were out of town for the weekend. Her mother had phoned the Townsend house before Jeff had managed to get her blouse entirely unbuttoned. A pregnant little pause settled over the long-distance telephone lines.

"Is this about your grandmother's house?" Lina finally asked.

"No." Tara shook her head firmly. "Definitely not."

"Oh." A disappointed tone crept into her mother's voice. "I was hoping you'd changed your mind about keeping your inheritance."

Tara figured she'd already inherited enough problems from her grandmother,

14

Brigid Delaney. "I told you, Mom, I don't want the house."

"Then why don't you sell it?"

Good question. And one Tara had asked herself at least once a day during the six months since her grandmother's sudden death.

"Are you going to be home this afternoon?" she asked suddenly.

"For my only daughter? Of course," Lina said without hesitation. "I'll make that marigold custard you like so well."

"That sounds wonderful."

Despite her uncharacteristic moodiness, Tara was smiling as she hung up the phone. Her mother might not resemble a typical American mom, and she definitely didn't bear the faintest resemblance to those early television mothers that showed up on late-night cable television, but the one thing Lina Delaney and Mrs. Cleaver had in common was the notion that there was no problem a home-baked dessert couldn't solve.

Five minutes later, as she pulled out of her driveway, Tara found herself wondering how Wally and the Beav would have handled having a white witch for a mother.

Gavin cursed as he passed Brigid Delaney's house on the way to the post office and saw that another window had been broken. Although he told himself that he should be grateful that breaking the windows of what was known as "the witch's haunted house" was as bad as juvenile crime got in Whiskey River, it still irritated him that the kids couldn't just go out to the dump and shoot at tin cans with BB guns like kids in other rural towns.

Over breakfast at the Branding Iron Café, Trace Callahan, Whiskey River's sheriff, suggested the logical solution. "I'll have J.D. board the windows up," he said as he dug into his Rustler's Special — steak, eggs and cottage fries.

"It shouldn't be the county's responsibility," Gavin said grumpily. "If Brigid's damn granddaughter would just do something with the house — move into it, sell it, burn it down, even — we wouldn't be having this discussion."

"Are you sure she's been notified?"

"I know Brigid's attorney sent official notification, then followed up with a bunch of letters. Hell, I wrote a couple myself. But there hasn't been any response."

"Maybe she's moved."

"Then the letters should come back."

"True." Trace considered that for a moment. "Maybe the county will take the

16

house over when she falls behind in her taxes. In the meantime, it's becoming a public nuisance. The closer we get to Halloween, the more likely it is that one of those kids is going to burn the place down. Since I want to avoid that, it only makes sense to have J.D. board up the windows. And bolt the doors."

"Bolts and boards aren't free. Last I heard the Mogollon County bookmobile was having to cut back on hours because of a lack of funds." He didn't mention sending in a sizable anonymous donation to keep that from happening.

Trace shrugged. "We've got some spare pieces of plywood hanging around after replacing the damage last month's storm did to the jail roof. No point in it going to waste. As for J.D., I don't think he'd mind doing the job off the books."

This was another thing Gavin liked about small towns. In the city, such a suggestion would call for innumerable oversight committees, public hearings, newspaper editorials and Lord knows what else. Here in Whiskey River, things were definitely more laid-back. The live-and-let-live attitude was one of the reasons he'd chosen to settle here.

"Thanks for the offer, but I don't mind

replacing the windows. Mostly I was just blowing off steam."

Trace eyed him over the rim of the coffee mug. "You know, Brigid Delaney's windows aren't your responsibility, either."

"That's what I keep telling myself," Gavin said.

"And?"

"And for some reason I can't make myself believe it."

"Maybe she cast a spell on you," Trace joked.

"That's one answer. Of course to believe it, I'd have to also believe that the old lady was a witch."

"So are you saying she was a fraud? Or a liar?"

"Neither. Not exactly." Gavin frowned into the thick black depths of his coffee as he framed his response. "I think she honestly believed that she possessed special powers. And from the business her mail-order herb catalog brought in, it's obvious a lot of other people around the country thought so, too. But I've just never bought into the notion of ghosts and goblins and things that go bump in the night."

"Yet the heroine of all your books is a witch."

Gavin was grateful when Trace referred

to them as books and not comics. Not many people bothered to make the distinction.

"I created Morganna to fill a niche," he said. "And to fill all those hours when I was behind bars." Gavin's scowl darkened as it always did when he thought back to his imprisonment. "Just when I thought for sure I'd go stir-crazy, I read about Wicca being one of the fastest growing religions in the country and decided to cash in on a trend."

And cash in he did. The success of Morganna, Mistress of the Night, had been nothing short of phenomenal.

"If you ask me," Trace said in a drawl that harkened back to the Texas roots he shared with Gavin, "Morganna's success has as much to do with her crime-fighting outfit as it does her sorcery."

Because the comment came from a man Gavin considered a good friend, a man whose dogged devotion to the truth had eventually earned him his freedom, Gavin didn't take offense. Especially since it happened to be true.

"Got a point there," he said agreeably. His quick grin faded as his thoughts returned to Brigid's house. "Although I never believed Brigid was a witch, unfortunately the kids in town do. Which is why they seem determined to break every window in the damn house."

"I wish I had the resources to put a man on the place for a few nights," Trace mused. "The problem with teenage vandalism is that it can lead down a rocky path straight to a jail cell."

Knowing that the former big-city cop had put in his own time on the wrong side of the bars in the juvenile justice system, Gavin figured Trace knew what he was talking about.

"You know," he said, "that's not a bad idea. I don't know why it didn't occur to me sooner." The more he thought about it, the more he liked it. "I could do that."

"Do what?"

"I could spend a couple of nights in the house. Wait for the kids to break a window, catch them in the act, then bring them to you for the scared-straight lecture."

Trace's expression was decidedly doubtful as he considered the proposed plan. "You're not talking about being armed or anything?"

"Hell, Trace, you know I've never owned any guns. I just want those kids to leave the old lady's house alone."

"I hadn't realized you were that close."

"Neither had I," Gavin admitted. "Until she was gone. Then I realized that somehow, when I wasn't looking, she became the closest thing to a real family I've had in years." He put some money on the table and stood. "Give Mariah a hug for me."

Trace smiled at the mention of his wife's name. Not a day went by that he didn't consider himself the luckiest man on the face of the planet to have had such a gorgeous, sexy, intelligent, talented woman fall in love with him.

"She's been away for four days wheeling and dealing in L.A., and as soon as she gets back tonight I intend to give her a lot more than a hug," he said. "But I doubt your name will come up."

Gavin laughed. "You're a lucky man, Trace."

"That's what Mariah keeps telling me." Trace grinned back. "You know, marriage isn't such a bad institution, pal."

"That's what *you* keep telling *me*. And call me crazy, but having already experienced life in an institution, I think I'll pass."

"I'm serious." Sober gunmetal gray eyes echoed Trace's words. "From what I can tell, you spend all your time working."

"When you love what you're doing, it isn't work," Gavin automatically responded with the answer he usually gave to interviewers who remarked on his apparent lack of any life outside his work.

"Yeah, I read that quote in *Newsweek*." Trace waved the words away with his left hand, his simple woven-gold wedding band gleaming in the buttery morning light. "I didn't buy it then and I don't now. The way it looks to me, all you've done is change your prison stripes for a denim jacket."

"What's that supposed to mean?"

"It means that the trappings may have changed. But although you've said that one of the reasons you came to Whiskey River was to enjoy life, you might as well still be spending your days behind bars."

Gavin frowned. "That's not a real attractive image you're painting there, Trace."

"If the boot fits," Trace said mildly. "Mariah has asked you to dinner six times in the past month. And each time you've said you had to work."

"I was up against a deadline."

"That's what you said. But you also just told me you mailed the new book off to your publisher this morning. So how about steaks tonight?"

"If Mariah's been in L.A. for four days, the last thing you two need is me crashing your reunion."

"Tomorrow, then."

"I have this idea I thought I'd flesh out. About Morganna taking on a bunch of gang bangers —"

"See. That's exactly what I'm talking about." Trace folded his arms and shook his head. "You just finished a project. What the hell would be wrong with taking a few days R and R to recharge the batteries?"

"And do what?"

"Hell, I don't know. Take up fishing."

"I hate fish. Catching them *and* eating them."

"Hiking, then. Or mountain climbing. Or go into Payson or Flagstaff and pick up a wild woman in some cowboy bar. When was the last time you got laid?"

Gavin took a moment to consider that question and realized that the fact that he couldn't remember was not a good sign.

"You've made your point. Maybe I will have dinner in Flagstaff tonight."

"Good." Nodding his satisfaction, Trace stood and tossed a few bills onto the table beside Gavin's. "Mariah will be glad to hear you're at least attempting to have some kind of social life. She worries about you."

"She's just like every other woman in the world," Gavin retorted as they left the café. "She can't bear to see an unmarried man running around loose."

"Believe me, pal," Trace said as he stopped beside his black-and-white Suburban with the Mogollon County seal on the door, "there's something to be said for spending your life in captivity with a gorgeous sexy woman."

"Ah, but that's my point. I do."

Trace laughed at the obvious reference to the fictional Morganna. "I was talking about a flesh-and-blood woman." He unlocked the door and climbed into the driver's seat. "Have fun tonight. You've earned a night on the town. Just don't try to drive back up that mountain after drinking. I'd hate to have to scrape you off the pavement."

"More than two beers and I'll crash in a motel. Or better yet, in some winsome young thing's bed."

"Always helps to keep a positive outlook," Trace agreed with a grin.

Gavin was walking across the parking lot when he heard Trace call out his name. He turned and saw that the sheriff had rolled down the driver's window. "What now?"

"Don't forget protection."

Gavin had a choice. He could be either annoyed or amused. He opted for amusement. "Yes, Mother."

2

The drive to her parents' home in Santa Cruz took only two hours, although Tara felt as if she were a time traveler, journeying back to the 1960s. Her parents lived in a commune that had been established by a group of counterculture rebels who'd found the San Francisco Haight-Ashbury hippie scene too commercially artificial for their tastes.

They'd been part of the small band of flower children who'd traveled down the coast, pooled their scant resources and bought a small dairy farm with the intention of using the proceeds from the milk and ice cream to fund their various artistic enterprises.

Serendipity had proven to be their ally. More than one of the commune members had achieved fame and fortune. Among the former residents was a world-famous balladeer, a Pulitzer prize-winning novelist and, of course her father, who could boast, if he were so inclined which he wasn't, that the past three First Ladies had been seen wearing bracelets fashioned in his work-shop.

And as if to prove that Mistress Fate did indeed have a sense of humor, last year Contented Cows, Inc. — specializing in dairy products from cows fed organically grown dandelions — had been purchased by C. S. Mackay Enterprises, which had allowed the band of former anticapitalists to pay off the mortgage on the two-hundred-acre site.

It was here Tara had grown up, one of several children granted a freedom unknown to the average kid in suburban America. During her preschool years, clothes had been optional, and although studies were never neglected, the teaching methods at the commune school had definitely not come from mainstream text-books.

Science had been more often than not taught outdoors, beneath the wide sky overlooking the sea. All those hours spent exploring tide pools and charting stars and Pacific storms and growing the gardens that supplied the extended family with vegetables had intensified Tara's affinity for nature.

Music and art were as important to the members of the small community as the air they breathed, and censorship, of course, was unheard-of. The commune library was extensive and varied, and was one of the reasons Tara's love of the written word had flourished.

Such a freewheeling atmosphere might be nirvana for someone wanting to grow up to be another Michelangelo or Georgette Heyer. A budding John Lennon or Bob Dylan would never lack for musicians to jam with. And there wasn't an adult in residence who wouldn't stop work to listen to a child's poem.

But Tara had always had the need for some boundaries in her life. She could still recall, vividly, when as a seven-year-old she had accompanied her parents to a Renaissance fair in Midland, Texas, and had been overwhelmed by the vastness of the country. The flat west Texas landscape, with its horizons stretching far in the distance on all four compass points, had made her feel as if she were adrift on a small dinghy in the middle of the ocean.

Later, she'd often felt exactly the same way living in the commune. While other teenagers all over the world were rebelling against authority, demanding freedom, Tara found the dictates of following one's own star unnerving.

The lack of boundaries had given her more than her share of anxiety attacks, and had definitely inhibited her social life. It was only when she'd discovered her love for mathematics, and the purity of numbers whose values never changed and always did what they were supposed to do — so long as you followed the rules and theorems — that she'd begun to feel comfortable.

From that day forward, she'd buried herself in her textbooks and, to the good-natured amusement of the adults in residence, had become the first math nerd in the artistic communal family.

Her mother was waiting for her outside the house her father had designed — a wonderfully sprawling series of cubes and towers perched on a rocky cliff overlooking the ocean. It was daring even for this community, and whenever anyone asked Darren McKenna what he would do when the house inevitably slid into the sea, he promptly answered, "Build another one, of course."

Her father never had been one to look beyond the moment. Which made him the opposite of his daughter, who could, with a quick glance at her leather-bound organizer, tell what she'd be doing at any given hour weeks into the future.

"Tara, darling." Her mother's flowing skirt swirled around her legs as she spanned the distance between them. "Welcome home. It's been too long."

As she returned her mother's embrace, Tara breathed in the scent of custom-blended jasmine and gardenia and felt instantly comforted.

"It's good to be here." It was true, Tara realized with some surprise. For the first time in as long as she could remember, she'd entered the gates with a sense of relief, a sense of homecoming.

Her mother leaned her head back and gave her a long maternal look that gave Tara the feeling that she could see all the way inside her. To her heart. Her soul.

"You haven't been sleeping well," Lina diagnosed.

"Now you're monitoring my dreams?" Tara tried for a friendly flippant tone and had to cringe when the words came out overly defensive.

"Actually, it was the shadows beneath your eyes that gave you away," Lina said mildly. "And the fact that you're too pale. Even for someone living in the city."

"I've always been fair skinned." Her ivory complexion had been the bane of her existence during her teenage years when she'd struggled to gain the golden tan the boys seemed to admire so on the other California girls.

"True. In that respect, as well as so many others, you take after your grandmother," Lina agreed. "But you've always had an inner glow." She reached out and trailed the back of her hand up Tara's cheek. "It's missing."

"It's only stress. One of my clients is a computer company that just completed negotiations for buying a software firm. I've been working nearly around the clock combing through years of back financial statements."

After graduating from Cal Poly University with an M.B.A., Tara had taken a top-level job in the financial department of a San Francisco Fortune 500 company. She'd continued to go to night school and had earned her C.P.A., but apparently she was more like her parents than she'd thought because she began to find the corporate atmosphere stifling. Eventually, she'd struck out on her own, becoming a consultant, and although she worked harder than she ever had as an employee, she enjoyed the ability to pick and choose her jobs.

"All the more reason to take a break and visit your mother." Although Lina's tone was characteristically mild, she could not keep the seeds of worry from her expressive hazel eyes.

"We'll have tea out on the patio. And we'll talk. About your work, your vacation. And whatever else you'd like."

"I definitely don't want to talk about Brigid's house."

"Of course you do, dear." Lina laced their fingers together and led Tara into the house. "That's why you're here."

Tara did not even try to argue. There was no need. Because, although she hadn't realized it until this moment, once again, her mother was right.

As she sat overlooking the sun-gilded waters and sipped a cup of lemon balm tea, and helped herself to a second helping of the smooth yellow custard made with crushed marigold petals from her mother's garden, Tara could literally feel the tension that had her shoulders tied up in knots slipping away.

"This is nice," she murmured, enjoying the sight of sea gulls diving for fish out amidst the breakers. "I hadn't realized how long it's been since I've taken a breather."

"You work too hard."

Tara knew her mother's comment was not criticism but merely observation. She opened her mouth to argue, but knew she could never lie to this woman.

"I know." She sighed. "But it's not as if I have a choice."

"We always have a choice, dear."

"That's easy for you to say," Tara flared, her nerves more on edge than she'd thought. "You dropped out thirty years ago. Some of us prefer life in the real world."

"Reality is where you find it, I suppose," Lina murmured, frustrating Tara even further.

As much as she truly loved her mother, she could not remember a single instance in her life when she'd been able to get a good argument going with her. Although Lina Delaney never withheld her feelings, neither would she try to force others into agreeing with her. She was, truly, a free spirit.

"Speaking of reality," Tara said, wanting to steer the subject away from her work, "I read in the paper that you've started working for the FBI."

Although her mother had never used her powers of second sight for profit, over the years stories of her psychic ability had become public knowledge. So much so that Lina's assistance was routinely requested by law enforcement officials who, while not exactly admitting belief, had solved more than one case with information given to them by Lina Delaney.

It was Lina's turn to sigh. Her gaze became distant as she looked out toward the horizon where a line of fishing boats trawled for tuna. "They thought I might be able to help them locate that serial killer who seems to be moving across the country."

"And?"

Lina briefly closed her eyes, as if to shut out the images she'd received from the evidence the police had collected in three western and two southern states. "I believe I may have provided some assistance."

Tara saw the pain etched in deep lines on her mother's tanned face. "I'm sorry." She reached out and took Lina's hand in hers. "It was rough, huh?"

"It wasn't pleasant." Lina linked their fingers together. "It also reminded me how very fortunate we are to have each other. All those young female victims had no one to care about them."

"Yes, they did." Tara squeezed her mother's hand. "They had you."

Lina smiled at that, a warm smile that for Tara had always been capable of soothing the cruelest of pains. "A bit late, I'm afraid," she said. "But thank you." Her expression sobered. "I know you said you don't want to talk about Brigid, but there's something I must tell you."

"What?" Tara asked with a sigh of resignation.

"I don't believe her death was from natural causes."

Tara felt the shock all the way through her body. "What do you mean? Surely she wouldn't have . . ."

"No. Of course your grandmother wouldn't have taken her own life. She relished every moment too dearly. But I've been receiving the most disturbing vibrations. And whenever I dream of the night she died, there's always a shadowy figure in the background. And a force so powerful it chills my blood."

Tara stared at her mother, unable to recall a single time she'd ever seen her looking so distraught. "I don't understand. With your gift —"

"You'd think I'd be able to see what happened, wouldn't you?" Lina broke in uncharacteristically. She shook her head. "I only see the shadow. Your father suggested it's because I'm too emotionally close to the situation."

"I suppose that makes sense," Tara allowed. "In fact, maybe the reason for the dreams in the first place is because you can't accept Brigid's death."

"I thought that might be the case, in the beginning. But now I don't think it is."

"Are you saying you think Brigid was murdered?"

"That sounds so overly dramatic, doesn't it? And murder is such an ugly word." Lina sighed. "Honestly, darling, I don't know what to think."

Neither did Tara. "I can't imagine anyone wanting to kill Grandy."

"I know. Everyone loved her so."

"And you told me the coroner ruled that she'd suffered a heart attack, which made her fall down the stairs." Tara still felt guilty for missing her grandmother's funeral. But a late-spring blizzard had kept her in Moscow, where she'd been helping a Russian-American entrepreneur open a pizza parlor.

"That was his official opinion. But I still can't shake the feeling that he was wrong. That being the case, I suppose I should be relieved you don't want to take possession of the house. I certainly wouldn't want something horrible happening to you, darling."

"You don't have to worry. The only thing I have to worry about is getting burned from too much Hawaiian sun."

Mother and daughter sat, hand in hand, watching as the blazing gold ball of sun dipped into the water, turning it a fiery crimson. Neither spoke. There was no need. As always, their thoughts were perfectly attuned.

Such was the legacy of the Delaney women. The legacy Tara had spent so many of her twenty-six years trying to escape. A legacy she feared, as she sat in the warming glow of the setting sun, she could no longer ignore.

All the way back to San Francisco she told herself that she was not going to Whiskey River. The town held too many painful memories for her. Besides, Brigid was dead. There wasn't any reason to return.

But then Tara thought of her mother's atypical anxiety, and although she was certain that the dreams were merely a manifestation of emotional loss, that didn't make them any less upsetting. Perhaps, Tara considered, the thing to do would be to put the house on the market and get rid of it once and for all. Then, maybe, her mother's mind could be at peace.

Knowing it was the right thing to do — the only thing she could do — Tara reluctantly called her travel agent and canceled her trip. Afterward, she unpacked all the beach and resort wear from her suitcases and tossed in some jeans and sweaters instead.

Then, frustrated but determined, she set the alarm in order to get an early start on the long, lonely drive to Arizona.

The inside of Brigid Delaney's house was, to put it charitably, a mess. A layer of dust covered everything like a ghostly shroud, spiders had taken up residence in all the corners of the ceiling, there was evidence that a family of mice had moved in and there were so many cobwebs draped over picture frames and chandeliers that Gavin felt as if he'd stumbled into Dickens's *Great Expectations*.

"Miss Faversham, I presume," he muttered, sweeping away a particularly thick cobweb hanging from a gilt-framed black-and-white photo of Brigid, clad in a wide straw hat and flower-sprigged cotton dress, gathering herbs in her garden.

The elderly woman he'd grown fond of had been striking. The young woman in the picture was a beauty. Her long wavy hair spilled from her straw hat like a rippling waterfall and her expressive, laughing eyes dominated a high cheekboned face.

Dress her in silks and satins and she could have been a princess. The amazing thing was that, although she'd had a presence that had reminded him of royalty, he'd never met a more down-to-earth woman in his life. Despite her distracting habit of insisting she was a witch.

"Dammit, Brigid." He glared at the photo as if its subject were capable of discerning his irritation, which, if even half her stories were to be believed, she just well might. "I'm doing my best here. But next time you decide to die and leave everything to a relative, couldn't you at least make certain the recipient is willing to accept the inheritance?"

He glanced around, depressed by the sight of the parlor that had always been cozy and tidy, looking so forlorn. Telling himself that he was only cleaning the place so he could spend the night in it without giving himself the creeps, he went out onto the service porch, gathered up a bucket and mop and set to work.

It was raining when Tara finally pulled into the driveway of her grandmother's home. Storms in Arizona's high country could be wild, and this one was no exception. Lightning flashed and thunder boomed like cannon fire. Wind wailed like the cries of lost souls in the treetops and drove the rain across the windshield of her sensible sedan with a force that had rendered visibility next to impossible as she'd driven the last thirty miles up the narrow, curving road to Whiskey River.

Then suddenly, a jagged bolt of lightning lit up the sky in a blinding white sulfurous flash, illuminating the house.

It hadn't changed. Tara didn't know why she thought it might have. Beneath the cloud white gingerbread trim, the fish-scale siding was still sky blue and the patterned windows flanking the arched front door were the same colored glass that Tara remembered gleaming like a princess's jewels when the morning sunlight streamed through them.

The copper roof of the tower had shone briefly in the bright light like a welcoming beacon and reminded her of summer tea parties she'd hosted for her grandmother and her dolls in that octagon-shaped room overlooking the garden.

This was the home where Brigid had given birth to her daughter, Lina, who, not wanting to break the chain of Delaney women, had kept her maiden name when she'd married, handing it down to her own daughter.

This was also the house where Brigid had soothed her granddaughter's broken heart after what Tara would always call the "Richard debacle." And proving that life was indeed made up of concentric circles, her grandmother had died here, as well. *Of an accident,* Tara thought firmly.

"Well, Grandy," she murmured as she looped her hands over the steering wheel and gazed at the house that was once again shrouded in rain and darkness, "you got your wish. I'm here. Although I'll be damned if I know why."

She took the key her grandmother's attorney had sent her out of her purse, then retrieved her overnight bag from the back seat. The larger bags in the trunk could wait until tomorrow.

She considered waiting a bit longer in hopes that the rain would at least slow down. But a glance up into a sky draped in black clouds assured her that the storm had stalled directly over Brigid's home.

"Nice welcome, Grandy. The least you could have done was use a few of your powers to turn off the waterworks."

She counted to three, then opened the car door and, holding her bag against her chest, made a dash for the front porch, which took longer than planned because she had to stop and unlatch the white picket gate.

By the time she reached the wide porch, she was drenched, and shivering. She'd forgotten how cold it could get in the mountains.

Beneath a winged griffin door knocker that had frightened Tara when she was a child was a shiny new doorknob. Wondering what had happened to the old hammered-brass handle she remembered having polished on more than one occasion, she managed to insert the key into the lock and was vastly relieved when it fit.

Just as she turned the knob, a clap of thunder shook the porch. An instant later she was blinded by a flash of brilliant white light. The acrid smell of sulfur assaulted her nostrils and a black veil drifted across her eyes.

Then Tara crumbled to the wooden floor beneath her feet.

Gavin, who had dozed off in a large wing chair positioned to give him a good view of the front windows, was jolted awake by the crack of thunder and almost simultaneous bolt of lightning. On some subconscious level, he'd been aware of a loud thud just after the lightning flash that had obviously struck very close to the house.

"All right!" It was what he'd been waiting for, an opportunity to catch the vandals in the act. He ran into the foyer and yanked open the ornately carved front door.

Instead of the teenage boys he'd thought he would find, Gavin found himself staring down at a seemingly lifeless form lying at his feet.

When another flash of lightning — thankfully more distant this time — lit up the sky, he stared in disbelief at a woman who could have stepped right out of that long-ago photograph of Brigid Delaney.

3

Tara had no idea how long she'd been unconscious. One minute she was standing on the familiar front porch fretting about a missing door handle, the next thing she knew she was in some man's arms, being carried into the darkened house. The house where her mother believed Brigid had been murdered!

"Put me down!" she demanded as she desperately tried to remember the self-defense training class she'd taken after nearly being mugged as she left her San Francisco office late one night.

"And have you swooning at my feet again?" Although the woman resembled a young Brigid Delaney, Gavin realized she had to be the granddaughter, the hotshot accounting whiz Brigid had boasted about.

"I didn't swoon." Tara glared up at him, frustrated when the deep shadows kept her from seeing his face. "I never swoon."

"Could've fooled me." Although it was not easy, maneuvering across the crowded room in the dark with a wiggling, angry woman in his arms, he managed to make his way to the red brocade chaise.

"If you're planning on raping me," Tara said between gritted teeth as she landed on the antique fainting couch with a bounce, "you should know that I've studied karate."

"Good for you." Gavin reached into the drawer of the papier-mâché table and pulled out the box of matches he knew Brigid kept there. Storms were a routine part of living in this remote corner of the state, making power outages commonplace. "Perhaps, after we get to know each other better, you can entertain me by breaking bricks with your bare hands."

The match flared as he struck it on the roughened side of the box, casting his face in an orange glow that made him look almost demonic. Her head still reeling, Tara tried to judge her chances for escape as he touched the match to the fat beeswax candle on the table.

"Who are you? And what are you doing in my grandmother's house?"

"I'm Gavin Thomas. The guy who sent you three separate letters wanting to know what the hell you wanted me to do with this place."

Sensing what they'd been about, and receiving disturbing vibrations from the envelopes that bore the bold masculine script, she had burned the letters without opening them.

"I don't recall receiving any letters." She lifted her chin and looked him right in the eye. "Obviously, the postman misdelivered them."

"Or you mistook them for junk mail and tossed them out," he said, deciding not to call her on the obvious lie. At least not yet.

"I suppose that's a possibility." Refusing to let him get the upper hand, she did not avert her gaze. Not even when his lips twitched and a wicked, knowing look came into his eyes. "If I *had* gotten the letters, what would they have said?"

"That I'd promised Brigid I'd look after the place until you arrived to take it off my hands. The last one mentioned, as politely as I could think to put it, that although I intended to do my best to live up to my word, I wasn't prepared to take on a lifetime commitment."

"Because you're not a man who enjoys commitment." It was not a question.

"You called that one right." The last time he'd allowed himself to get seriously involved with a woman, he'd ended up in prison. Gavin was not eager to repeat either experience.

"Yet my grandmother still entrusted you with her house."

He shrugged his shoulders. "I tried to tell her I wasn't the stick-around type. She didn't believe me."

"My grandmother was infamous for her ability to only see what she wanted to see." Tara decided, for discretion's sake, not to mention that Brigid's intuitive sense of people was very seldom off the mark. "You haven't answered my second question," she reminded him. "What are you doing here in the middle of the night?"

"I was sleeping. Until you woke me up by collapsing on the porch."

Tara rubbed her temple where a headache was pounding. "I don't understand what happened."

"From the crack that woke me up, and the sulfur smell when I opened the door, I'd say lightning struck close by. Probably one of the trees. I'll check in the morning. I'd guess that the force knocked you down." Leaning down, he brushed away the auburn hair that had fallen over her forehead and examined a rapidly growing lump.

When his fingertips stroked her skin with

a slow touch that was meant to be soothing but in reality was anything but, Tara jerked her head away. "I suppose I should count myself lucky I wasn't hit myself."

"Definitely."

The air around them grew thick with the scents of rosemary and yarrow emanating from the burning candle. Rosemary, Tara remembered, was used to weave a spell of remembrance, and love. As for the yarrow, Brigid had told her that if you put a sachet of it beneath your pillow, you would dream of your true love.

"You should probably get out of those wet clothes," Gavin said when Tara began to shiver. "Before you catch cold."

She was wearing a blouse the color of a buttermilk biscuit tucked into a pair of snug jeans.

"Good try, Mr. Thomas. But I'm not that naive." Nor foolhardy.

"The name's Gavin. And believe me, sweetheart, I was only trying to keep you from catching cold."

The sparring helped. Helped clear her head and calm her nerves. "Aren't you considerate?"

"That's me," he agreed with equal sarcasm. "Mr. Consideration."

She should have been irritated. Instead,

dammit, she was undeniably interested. "Well."

She took a deep breath, then wished she hadn't as she watched his steady gaze slip from her face to her breasts. She glanced down and realized the tailored silk blouse that appeared so staid when worn with her oatmeal-hued suit in the office had suddenly become far too revealing for comfort.

The material was clinging to her breasts like a second skin and her nipples had pebbled — from the cold, she assured herself — and were pressing against the wet silk in a way guaranteed to instill dangerous thoughts in just about any man.

"On second thought, I think I will change my clothes."

"Good idea." His unenthusiastic tone said otherwise. Although he truly didn't want to be responsible for her catching pneumonia, Gavin found himself more than a little reluctant to surrender the view. When his gaze returned to her face and he viewed her poisonous glare, he knew she'd been reading his thoughts.

Since he was not accustomed to apologizing for being either human or male, he gave her wet shoulder a fraternal pat.

"Your overnight bag is still on the porch. I'll go get it."

He was back in a moment.

She'd managed, during that brief interlude, to regain a bit of composure. And caution. "If you don't mind, Mr. Thomas, I'd like to see some identification."

"I was wondering when you were going to think of that." He reached into his back pocket, pulled out his billfold and handed it over. "You'll find an Arizona driver's license, American Express card, a couple of Visas and a Mogollon County library card. That should convince you I'm who I say I am."

She glanced through the plastic-encased cards and lingered momentarily over one, thinking that it was unfair for any mere mortal to look so sexy in a driver's license photo. His dark hair, swept back from his forehead, was disgustingly thick, his hooded eyes were so darkly brown as to be almost black and his jaw could have been chiseled from granite. She decided that the cleft in that square chin was definitely overkill.

"You seem to be who you say you are," she agreed. "But that still doesn't mean I can trust you."

"Your grandmother entrusted her house to me," he said pointedly. "And there's a letter waiting for you on the upstairs dresser that will undoubtedly vouch for me, as well."

"She left a letter? For me?"

"It's got your name on the envelope."

"Why didn't you send it to me?"

"Because I had my own letter instructing me to leave it for you to read when you arrived. Besides," he pointed out, "it's a good thing I didn't forward it, since all my other letters appear to have gotten lost."

Once again his tone told her that he knew she'd been lying. She would have been uncomfortable about that had her mind not latched on to another thought.

"Don't you think that's strange? Her death was so sudden, but she'd already written letters to both of us to be read after her death?"

"I did in the beginning. But then I decided she was just one of those people who likes to plan ahead. I've heard of people leaving instructions with their lawyers. Or letters in safe-deposit boxes."

"I suppose that makes sense," Tara allowed. "Since you were included, you must have been close to her."

He shrugged. "She was lonely." His tone was edged with a hint of censure she tried to ignore. "She didn't have any family in Whiskey River, and I was a stranger here, as well. So, I guess you could say we kind of adopted each other."

"Did she happen to mention to you what she did for a living?" Tara's voice held an unmistakable challenge.

"You're not talking about her mail-order herbal business."

She folded her arms across her chest and met his gaze with a long, level look of her own. "No, I'm not."

"She told me she was a witch. Since the fantasy seemed harmless enough, I didn't let it bother me."

"How open-minded of you." She reached out and took the gray overnight case from his hand. "And for the record, Mr. Thomas," she said as she headed toward the doorway and the stairs that led to her grandmother's bedroom, "it wasn't any crazy old lady's fantasy. My grandmother was a genuine, card-carrying, crystal-gazing, spell-casting, druidic witch."

That said, she swept from the room, leaving Gavin to wonder if lunacy ran through the genes of all the Delaney women. Or just the gorgeous ones.

Her grandmother's bedroom was just as she remembered it. Cabbage flowers bloomed on the yellowed ivory wallpaper and the antique sleigh bed was covered by a quilt that had been in the family for generations. Celtic animals and geometric patterns echoed the stone carvings and metalwork of that ancient time.

She found the letter on the dresser, just as the annoying man downstairs had told her. The handwriting was a bit more spidery than she remembered, but there was no doubt that it was her grandmother's. And even if she hadn't recognized the delicate script, the energy emanating from the ivory envelope was unmistakable.

The paper was handmade, speckled with dried flowers and herbs from the garden, and carried the familiar lavender scent that Tara had always associated with Brigid. She inhaled the evocative fragrance and sighed.

"I'm sorry, Grandy," she said softly. "I should have been here for you. In the end." Instead, she'd continually put off her grandmother's requests that she visit, leaving a lonely old woman to befriend the man downstairs. A man who was not only a stranger, but an obvious disbeliever, as well.

Feeling horribly guilty, Tara sat down on the thick feather mattress and began to read.

Dearest Tara,

If you're reading this, it means you've overcome your reluctance to return to your roots, at least temporarily. And although I have always understood your need to follow your own spiritual path, it saddens me that past circumstances have caused you to view the gifts you've inherited as a curse, rather than a blessing.

I realize how difficult this journey has been for you, darling Tara. And just as I cannot erase the pain you've suffered, neither can I promise instant miracles.

But what I do promise is this — if you stay beneath this roof for one cycle of the moon, your life will inexorably change. At the end of this time you'll be able to put the past behind you and move on.

You've already made the first step, Tara. Now I'm asking you to trust in your grandmother, who loves you, one last time. I promise you will not be disappointed. Blessed be.

The traditional words of farewell blurred through the mist of tears gathering in Tara's eyes. She had to blink to clear her vision in order to read the PS.

I know Gavin Thomas is not the type of man you're accustomed to. But since his arrival in Whiskey River, he's come to mean a great deal to me. In fact, I consider him almost like family. It would please me very much if you could open your heart to him, if only as a friend. His own road has not been an easy one. I believe you may find you both have much in common.

"Dammit, Grandy," Tara muttered, "this really is dirty pool. Even for you."

She glared up at a needlepoint-framed photo of her grandmother and was struck by a resemblance she'd never before noticed. Except for the fact that she had a time-saving, no-fuss haircut, she could have been looking in a mirror.

"I cannot believe that you're asking me to give up my life in San Francisco to move in here for a month, befriend an obvious nonbeliever, come to grips with my past and, oh, yes — you're not fooling me for a minute here — in my spare time I'm supposed to fall in love with your precious Mr. Thomas, which isn't going to happen because I'd rather kiss a toad."

As if possessing an energy all its own, the lie reverberated around the room until she could practically feel it bouncing off all the flowered walls. Tara closed her eyes and shook her head. It was impossible. She simply couldn't do it. Whiskey River held too many painful memories.

The thing to do was to spend the night here, since the idea of driving back down that twisting mountain road in the dark was less than appealing. By tomorrow morning, the storm would have passed and she could go to Kauai as originally planned, where she would spend the rest of the days she'd allotted for her vacation basking in the sun before returning to her uncomplicated life.

As impossible as others might find it, Tara could actually hear her grandmother's voice challenging that last thought.

"All right. So, in this case, uncomplicated may translate to boring," she allowed. "But it's what I like."

It was also, she admitted as she changed into dry clothes, what she needed. A boring, predictable, *normal* life.

She left the bedroom on her usual brisk, efficient stride determined to send Mr. Gavin Thomas back to wherever it was he'd come from.

Gavin had just started a fire in the stone fireplace when he heard her coming back down the stairs and inwardly cursed Brigid — not for the first time — for getting him involved with her house. And as if broken windows and juvenile vandals weren't enough, he now had her ill-tempered granddaughter to deal with.

"I thought you might have left already," she said pointedly.

There was no way he was going to leave her alone in this house, without power or a telephone, with those potential juvenile delinquents running loose, but Gavin decided to save the argument until he learned her plans.

"Actually, I was waiting around to hear the verdict. So what is it? Are you going to stay?"

"Not that it's any of your business. But no. I'm not."

He nodded. "I figured that would be your decision."

"Now you're a mind reader?"

"No. But I am pretty good at reading people. It only makes sense that if you had any deep feeling for the place, you would have come home before now."

While your grandmother was still alive. He didn't say the words out loud, but Tara heard them, just the same.

"Since you don't know anything about

me, it's a bit presumptuous of you to pretend to understand my reasons for staying away."

"Ah, but there's where you're wrong." A log shifted, sending a shower of sparks up the chimney. He took a black iron poker and began rearranging the wood. "As it turns out, I know a great deal about you."

"From my grandmother." It was not a question.

"She talked a lot about you," he agreed as he worked on getting the burning logs where he wanted them. "I figured a lot of the business and school stuff was typical grandmother bragging. But I was referring to more personal things."

"Such as?"

He replaced the poker and turned toward her once again, enjoying the way her lips had formed into a sexy pout. "Such as the fact that part of the reason for your career success is that you threw yourself into your work after being stood up at the altar by that hotshot Montgomery Street lawyer."

Ignoring her sudden sharp intake of breath, he crossed the room, picked up a bottle of brandy he'd brought with him and poured the amber liquor into two Irish crystal balloon glasses.

"She had no right to tell you about that."

"Brigid worried about you. She thought you needed a man in your life." He held one of the glasses out to her.

Tara took a sip of the brandy in an attempt to soothe her ragged nerves. Although it was smooth as velvet, and warmed her all the way to her toes, it did nothing to instill calm. Deciding the only way to tackle a man like Gavin Thomas was head-on, she tossed up her chin, determined to put a stop to this right now. Before it got out of hand.

"For your information, Mr. Thomas —"

"It's Gavin," he corrected.

"For your information," she began again, "I have men in my life. Lots of men. More than I can keep track of."

"Tara, Tara." Gavin clucked as he shook his dark head with feigned disappointment. "What would your grandmother say if she could hear you telling such bald-faced lies?"

"I'm not —"

"Of course you are," he smoothly overrode her protest yet again. "Look at you." He eyed her over the rim of his glass. "You're a lovely woman, but you insist on hiding any feminine attributes beneath that oversize shirt and baggy jeans."

She wished they'd never gotten on to the unpalatable subject of her love life. Or lack of it. She also wished he'd button his own damn shirt. His chest, gleaming copper in the flickering firelight, was unreasonably distracting.

"Excuse me." Frost tinged her voice, her eyes. "Perhaps I should go upstairs and change into my red lace teddy and hooker high heels."

Oddly enough, although she was practically spitting ice chips at him, Gavin was enjoying himself. "As appealing as that might be, it would also be a bit intimate. Since we've just met. But you could loosen up just a little."

He tossed back the brandy, then closed the gap between them. "Unbutton a couple of buttons so the collar isn't choking you to death." Without asking permission, he did exactly that. When his fingers brushed the skin framed by the now-open neck of her white blouse, Tara stiffened. "And next time tell the cleaners to go easier on the starch." He frowned at the stiff pleated front. "A bulletproof vest would probably be softer than this."

Her fingers tightened around the stem of her glass. "My choice of clothing is none of your business."

"I suppose that's true. In theory." Gavin rubbed his chin. "But it offends my artistic sensibilities to see a woman working overtime to hide her beauty."

Before she could respond to that outrageous statement, a sudden crash shattered the silence, followed by the sound of breaking glass.

4

Tara screamed as the glass from the leaded front window came flying into the room.

Gavin shouted a raw, pungent curse and tore out of the room. She heard the front door open, heard his footfalls as he ran across the front porch. Her first coherent thought was that her grandmother was playing a trick from the world beyond. But blowing in windows wasn't Brigid's style.

She'd be more likely to call down the moon than try to terrify her granddaughter into a man's arms. Then Tara spotted the rock lying on the flowered carpet, a rock she knew that had landed there not by magic, but by very mortal means.

Suddenly concerned that Gavin was putting himself in danger just to impress her, she took off after him and arrived at the front door just as he was dragging two obviously terrified boys up the porch steps by their shirt collars.

"My cellular phone is on the table in the kitchen," he told her. "Call 9-1-1 and have the sheriff come out and pick these two up for vandalism."

"It wasn't vandalism," the larger of the boys insisted. "Not exactly."

Gavin shook him. "Look, kid. You purposefully broke a window, just for the hell of it. What would you call it?"

"A dare," the other boy insisted in a voice that sounded perilously close to tears. "Eddie Rollins double dog dared us to break the window. Said we didn't have the nerve."

"Since when does it take any nerve to throw a rock through the window of an abandoned house?" Gavin demanded.

"It takes a lot of guts," the other boy insisted. " 'Cause everybody knows the Delaney place is haunted."

"You sure about that?"

"The old lady was a witch," the boy answered. "Makes sense it'd be haunted."

"Haunted or not, it doesn't give you the right to go destroying property that isn't yours." He tossed them onto the porch swing. "Don't move." Then he looked up at Tara. "I thought you were going to call the sheriff."

"Do you really think that's necessary?" she asked, glancing at the two boys who were trying to look rebellious, although it was obvious that they were scared to death of this furious, glowering man.

"Dammit, lady, in case it escaped your attention, there's glass all over your grandmother's parlor floor. If you'd been another foot closer to that window, you could have some of those shards embedded in your face."

"I certainly wouldn't have enjoyed that." She folded her arms and studied the two young vandals again. "But I'm not certain that it's necessary to involve the sheriff."

"They've been pulling stunts like this for the past six months. It's gotten damn expensive replacing the windows and I think it's time they acted more responsibly."

"I'm all for responsibility." She paused. Her eyes slanted, she rocked back on her heels and chewed thoughtfully on a thumbnail. "But I believe that, along with having them pay for the damage, we can take care of this little problem ourselves, Gavin."

A ghost of a smile played at the corners of her lips. "Did I mention that I inherited many of my grandmother's powers?"

As angry as he was, Gavin couldn't help smiling as he followed her train of thought. "Actually, I don't believe that came up."

"Well, although they've definitely proven

to be a mixed blessing, I did. Which I suppose, if one wants to be annoyingly technical, makes me a witch, as well." She flashed the boys the type of spellbinding trust-me smile that Gavin figured the wicked witch had used to lure Hansel and Gretel into her gingerbread cottage.

"I'm afraid I'm flat out of eye of newt, but I believe I saw some goat's blood in the refrigerator. And some dried rattlesnake skin. And, of course, grandmother always kept chicken entrails in the freezer for just such occasions."

She nodded, satisfied. "Yes, I think there are enough supplies on hand to weave a lovely black spell." She leaned down and ran her hand over the top of the older boy's head, ruffling his dark hair. "How would you like to be turned into a lizard?"

She flashed another smile as she turned to his companion. "With your pointy little ears, I rather see you as a bat," she decided. "Tell me, dear —" she trailed her hand down the side of his face "— are you afraid of the dark?"

"Of course he's not," Gavin said, getting into the spirit of things. "After all, he's running around out here in the woods in the middle of the night. I'd say he's probably part night creature already."

"That was my impression, as well," Tara agreed. "So it's settled." She rubbed her hands together gleefully. "I do so love turning people into reptiles. And it's been ages since I turned any boy into a bat." She sighed. "I'd almost forgotten how much fun it is."

"Want me to go light the Black Sabbath candles?" Gavin suggested.

"Thank you, Gavin. I'd appreciate the assistance. Oh, and if you wouldn't mind, could you please get my cauldron down from the top shelf in the kitchen?"

"No problem."

"Fine. Then we can get started. Ready for an adventure, boys?" She reached out, as if to take their hands.

"Well," Gavin said as the boys streaked past them as if the devil himself were on their tails, "I'd say you settled that little problem. Although it's a good thing you're not going to stay. Because by this time tomorrow the word will be all over the country that Brigid Delaney's granddaughter is a witch."

"Perhaps I'll have to tune-up my broomstick and buzz the courthouse before I leave."

She was kidding, Gavin reassured himself as he followed her into the house. It was just a joke. Like the one she'd played on those kids.

Tara was standing in the middle of the rug, looking down at the pieces of broken glass. "It's going to be difficult cleaning this up in the dark. I suppose it can wait until morning."

"That'd probably be best," he agreed. "There's some plywood outside in the back. I'll nail it over the window until I can replace the glass tomorrow. Luckily, I'm getting pretty handy at this."

She glanced up at him with a surprise that he did not think was feigned. "Then you were telling the truth earlier? This happens often?"

"Often enough." He rubbed his jaw. "You really didn't read my letters, did you?"

"No."

"Any special reason?"

"I don't know." She sighed as she decided there was no point in trying to convince him that they'd all gotten lost in the mail. "It's difficult to explain."

Gavin didn't press her for an explanation. She didn't sound all that eager to unburden herself, and frankly, he didn't care why she'd chosen to stay away from Whiskey River.

"Relationships can get a little sticky in the best of families," he said mildly.

"You can say that again."

She appeared small and pale and vulnerable in the muted glow of the fireplace. Something stirred inside Gavin, something that felt uncomfortably like sympathy. Remembering all too well the last time he'd made the mistake of comforting a troubled female, he tamped down the feeling.

"I'd better go get that plywood."

She'd sensed his interest. And his caution. She nodded, relieved he'd chosen to avoid the issue, but wondered at the edge of anger she thought she detected in his tone.

"Thank you." She glanced around, noticing that the room didn't look half-bad considering the house had been vacant for six months, and wondered how it would look in the bright light of day. "I'll want to repay you for all your work."

"That's not necessary. It wasn't that big a deal."

"To me it is. You've done me an immense favor. It would be a great deal more difficult to sell the house if it'd been badly vandalized."

"You're selling?"

He should have expected it, Gavin told

himself. Especially when she didn't care enough to show up for her grandmother's funeral. But for some reason, he didn't like the idea of a stranger moving into Brigid's house.

"I don't see that I have any choice."

"Everyone has choices," he argued, unknowingly echoing Lina Delaney.

"Of course you're right." She lifted her chin, daring him to challenge the decision that had not come easily. "And since my work is in San Francisco and the demands of my career preclude my having a second home, *my* choice is to sell the house and invest the funds in my IRA."

Gavin wondered if she knew exactly how much she resembled her grandmother when she stuck her chin out like that. Despite the fact that she'd been nearly three times his age, Brigid had been the most appealing — and frustrating — woman he'd ever met. And now it appeared that Tara had inherited both her appeal and her tenacity.

"I never knew a witch with a retirement account."

"Known many witches have you, Mr. Thomas?"

"Gavin," he reminded her yet again. "And your grandmother was the only one. That I know of."

69

"Well, now you know two." She flashed him a smile. "And this one definitely believes in financial planning."

That siren's smile, which he knew to be as fake as her alleged eye of newt, reached her eyes, making them gleam like emeralds in the shimmering candlelight. When he found himself unreasonably tempted to kiss her, Gavin decided it was definitely time to call it a night.

"It's late," he said when the green lacquered long-case clock suddenly announced the hour with a silver-belled minuet rather than the expected peal of chimes. "If you've been driving all day, you've got to be exhausted. Why don't you go on up to bed, and I'll fix the window."

The soft feather bed was undeniably appealing. However . . .

"I don't mind waiting until you're finished."

"I'm not going to attack you, Tara."

Tara wondered what she'd said to earn such a dark and deadly look. "I didn't think you were. It's just that I wouldn't feel right leaving you with all this work."

Gavin reminded himself that if she'd never heard of him, she couldn't know about his admittedly unsavory past. "I told you, I've gotten it down to a science. Go to bed. I'll lock up and sack out on the couch, in case those kids come back."

"As much as I appreciate the offer, it's definitely not necessary for you to stay. I may as well get used to being alone."

"I thought you were going to sell the house." He'd assumed she'd list it in the morning, then hightail it back to her safe, comfortable, predictable life in San Francisco.

"I am. But surely Brigid told you about the condition she put on my bequest?"

"She told me she was leaving the place to you. And she asked me, if anything ever happened to her, to look out for it until you arrived. That's all."

She gave him a long look and determined he was telling the truth. "Although Brigid believed in people following their own stars, she never believed me when I told her that the life I've chosen is the one I truly want.

"So she stipulated that before I can sell the house, I have to live in it. For a month."

"A month?"

"Thirty days to be exact."

"Thirty days. Imagine that." Things were definitely going to get interesting around Whiskey River, Gavin decided.

"Interesting doesn't even begin to describe the possibilities, Mr. Thomas."

Her smile at his surprise that she'd discerned his thoughts was cool and knowing. Gavin found it irritating as hell. "You didn't read my mind. You just made an obvious assumption and got lucky."

"Whatever you say," she answered pleasantly. Then, possessing a bit of her grandmother's flair for the dramatic, she decided that it was time to exit the scene.

"I'm suddenly very tired. I believe I *will* go to bed. Good night Mr. Thomas. Please remember to lock up when you leave."

As she entered the bedroom, she stopped in front of the photograph of Brigid. "Good try, Grandy," she murmured. "And I'll admit he's sexy, in a kind of rough and dangerous sort of way, but I'm not going to let myself get involved."

Ten minutes later, after brushing her teeth and washing her face, Tara slipped between the flowered sheets and the antique quilt. When the scent of yarrow wafted up from the goose-down pillow, she tossed it onto the floor, squeezed her eyes shut tight and vowed that she was *not* going to dream of Gavin Thomas.

Despite her best intentions, the vow was broken as soon as she drifted off to sleep.

72

It was the sound that woke her. Tara froze, willing her body to remain absolutely still while her mind, lagging behind, struggled to leave the misty, sensual dream.

Her heart was pounding so hard and so fast in her ears she had to strain to hear the sound. But there it was, a strange scratching noise at the window that reminded her of a movie she'd seen on late-night cable last week. Dracula, she remembered, had made that same sound against the glass just before flying into his victim's bedroom.

Don't be ridiculous, she scolded herself. *That was only a movie.*

She slipped from between the tangled sheets. Although she assured herself that it was only her overstimulated imagination, she refrained from turning on the bedside lamp for fear of drawing attention to herself. She padded stealthily to the window in her bare feet, took a deep breath and jerked the curtain back.

Then laughed as relief flooded over her.

"It's only a tree branch, dummy. Scraping against the window. Geez, you'd think you'd never spent a night alone."

Feeling much better, Tara went back to

bed. As she drifted back to a sleep filled with Gavin Thomas, she didn't hear the faint creaking of floorboards over her head.

In the morning, Tara was relieved to discover that Gavin had obviously gone back to wherever it was he lived after boarding up the window. After a restless night, filled with vivid, disturbingly sensual dreams, having to face him first thing in the morning would have been too much to handle.

She searched the cupboards, frustrated but not surprised when all she could find were the herbal teas her grandmother had so successfully marketed through various catalogs. And as much as she had enjoyed the lemon balm tea with her mother the other day, what she needed now was a strong jolt of caffeine to rid her mind of cobwebs and lingering thoughts of a man she had no intention of becoming involved with.

Despite her grandmother's interference.

Deciding the only thing to do was get dressed and go into town for coffee at the Branding Iron Café before meeting with Brigid's lawyer, she went back upstairs to take a shower.

"I realize your talents far surpass mine, Grandy," she muttered out loud as she blew her hair dry. "But if I wanted to, I could cast a spell of my own. To counter yours.

"Of course that's also what you want me to do, isn't it?" Tara frowned at her reflection in the wavy bathroom mirror. "That's what all this is about. You've brought me back here to force me to get in touch with my roots. Well, I've got news for you, Grandy. I'm not going to cast any spells. I've made a life for myself that doesn't involve magic. I'm happy."

The falsehood hung in the air, mocking her. "All right, perhaps *satisfied* is a better word. But it's only because I've had a grueling year. By the time I leave here, I'll be itching to get back to work."

Back to her tax tables and interest rates and stock indexes. Back to her tidy apartment on Russian Hill, decorated with no-nonsense Scandinavian furniture, where she spent her nights and weekends laboring over computer spreadsheets.

"I've worked hard to get where I am," she insisted as she marched into the bedroom and for the second time that morning almost tripped over the suitcases that had not been there when she'd gone to bed last night.

The idea that Gavin had brought them

75

up while she'd been sleeping, had invaded her bedroom and watched her, made her blood boil. She was going to give him a piece of her mind, Tara vowed.

Just as soon as she had her coffee.

It was not surprising to Tara that the café had not changed during her years away. The plastic cow waiting to be branded still stood on the flat roof. Inside, the tables were still Formica, the booths red vinyl and red-and-white gingham curtains framed windows decorated with cardboard cutouts of broom-riding hags, grinning orange pumpkins and cartoonlike skeletons. Men in baseball caps and Stetsons sat at the counter hunkered over their cups of coffee. Two of the booths were taken up by older couples, another by an elderly man with a thick snowy beard.

Tara's entrance caused a notable stir. She could feel the eyes of the other patrons on her as she made her way to a back booth.

"Hi, Tara," the owner of the café greeted her as she filled the heavy white coffee mug and put a laminated menu on the table. "Welcome back. It's been a long time."

"Yes. It has." Tara took a careful sip of

the steaming coffee. It was black and strong.

"I was real sorry when Brigid passed on. She was a nice lady."

"Yes, she was." Tara had never understood people who could be chatty in the morning. She took another longer drink of coffee and willed the caffeine to enter her bloodstream.

Iris Johnson leaned forward to keep her next words from being overheard. "You know, your grandmother was responsible for my third marriage."

"Really." Tara tried to appear interested, although she knew it really didn't matter. The café owner was obviously tickled to have a new audience for her story.

"Lyle and I were high school sweethearts. But my mama and daddy thought he was too wild, so I ended up marrying Joe Porter. Who was a darling, and we had six terrific kids together. But he never made my heart race like Lyle could. Know what I mean?"

Tara instantly thought of Gavin Thomas standing in front of the fire with his shirt unbuttoned. "Yes, I think I get the drift."

"Well, Joe passed away about two years ago, about the time you were supposed to get married to that doctor fellow —"

"He was an attorney," Tara corrected without thinking.

"That's right." Iris nodded. "I remember thinking that a big-city lawyer should know something about breach of promise."

Despite her discomfort with the way the conversation had suddenly veered off course, Tara found herself speculating about how her filing such an outdated lawsuit would have gone over in Richard's uptown law firm. Especially when he'd been so concerned about making partner.

The partnership, she remembered all too correctly, he'd feared he would lose if anyone found out that he'd married a witch.

"You were saying?" she prompted, wanting to return the topic to its original track.

"Oh, yeah. Well, anyway, I missed my Joe so much, I married this slick guy who drove into town in a flashy Ford Thunderbird and promised to make me his queen."

The frown on the woman's face suggested that had definitely not been a match made in heaven. "I take it that didn't work out."

"After he managed to fleece me outta my nest egg, I discovered he already had six other wives scattered over three states."

"That's terrible!"

"Could've been worse if I'd given him half interest in the Branding Iron, like he'd wanted," Iris said pragmatically. "Fortunately, Trace — he's the sheriff here, a great guy, you'll like him a lot — was suspicious and ran a check on him before I could sign the final papers.

"Well, you can understand how after that close call, I'd about decided to give up on men altogether."

"I know the feeling," Tara murmured.

"I figured you might," Iris said with a nod. "Anyway, then Lyle's wife, Edith, passed on. That's when I decided to take the bull by the horns and visit Brigid."

"Who gave you a love potion," Tara guessed.

"She had me stand in front of the mirror every morning and every night and recite three new things I liked about myself each time. Said it wasn't really a spell, but more of a self-confirmation. That before someone could love me, I needed to be able to love myself.

"At first I thought it was foolish. Like some of that new-age self-help stuff. But I'll admit that my self-esteem had taken a battering from that rat of a bigamist, so I think your grandmother was right to remind me that I had some things going for me."

"My grandmother was a very wise woman."

"That's sure enough true. After two weeks of that, she told me to hang one of those wind chimes on my front porch where the west wind would blow, and gave me some words to say each morning. And she gave me a lodestone to carry in my pocket."

She reached into the pocket of her black skirt and pulled out a small, dark, outwardly unremarkable stone. "Said I should touch it several times a day and think of my Lyle."

Her weatherworn face softened. "I didn't have this stone more than a week when Lyle came into the café and ordered the Rustler's Special. That's the Number Four. Steak, two eggs, cottage fries and toast.

"Well, when I was handing over the plate of whole-wheat toast our fingers touched, and it was like a shock of electricity just shot through the both of us. Made me drop the plate and the toast fell right onto his lap. Jelly side down.

"But you know, Lyle didn't even seem to notice. We just kept looking at each other, and right then and there I knew that Brigid had made all my dreams come true."

Tara smiled. "That's a nice story."

"Isn't it?" Iris sighed happily. "We were married down at the Healing Waters Baptist Church six weeks later. Course I never did tell Lyle what brought him into the Branding Iron that morning. And I keep the stone in my pocket. Just to make sure he sticks around."

Her eyes looked misty and reminiscent, making Tara afraid that she might start weeping when a red truck driving past the window caught Iris's attention.

"Did your grandmother tell you about Gavin Thomas?"

"No. But we've met. Apparently he's been looking after her house."

"Tryin' to, anyway," Iris said. "He and Brigid got to be really good friends, which, of course, didn't surprise me, since Brigid took to just about everybody. Although some of the people in town worried about her getting mixed up with a convicted felon."

An icy chill skimmed up Tara's spine. "A felon?" she asked, trying to keep her voice from betraying her distress. She thought again of her mother's belief that Brigid's death was not an accident.

"He did time for murder in Texas."

Murder. The ugly word tolled in her head

like a death knell. "Are you sure about that?" Tara knew, all too well, how fast gossip spread in a small town, and how easily facts became twisted.

"Apparently he killed the woman he was having an affair with," Iris divulged, her eyes brightening as she realized that she was the first person in Whiskey River to pass on this particularly sordid little story. "A married woman. Who was pregnant, to boot."

Tara found it difficult to believe that the man who'd boarded up her grandmother's windows and helped her play a trick on those teenagers had committed such a horrendous crime.

"Are you certain? Wouldn't he be in prison?"

"Trace — that's the sheriff —" Iris reminded Tara, "was a police officer in Dallas before moving here. Word is that he found some evidence that got Gavin out of prison on some kinda legal technicality."

"I see." But she didn't. Not at all. "He killed his lover?" And she'd gone to bed with him still in the house? Boy, that was a real smart move!

"His married lover," Iris repeated. "Not that I much blame the woman for letting him park his boots beneath her bed. He's a handsome devil. I can't picture many women bein' able to resist those dark and dangerous charms."

Tara was about to say that she could certainly think of one, when a trucker in a denim shirt and a black Oakland Raiders cap called out for a refill.

"Well, I've done enough jawing for one morning," Iris said, returning to being the brisk café owner who managed to keep a steady procession of orders coming out of the kitchen.

"I'd better get back to work and let you figure out what you want. You can't go wrong with the pecan sticky buns," she suggested. "I don't want to blow my own horn, but there are those who think that the Branding Iron serves the best sweet rolls in the state."

"The sticky buns sound great."

"You got it." She picked up the menu with a satisfied nod and hurried away to make the rounds of the tables refilling cups. That accomplished, she returned with a chipped plate of warm sticky caramel buns studded with pecans.

"I forgot to ask," Iris said, "are you planning to live here and take on your grandmother's mail-order business?"

"No." Tara managed a tight, polite smile.

"Actually, I'll be staying in the house this month. But then I'm selling it, and returning to my own home."

"That'd be in Frisco."

"San Francisco. That's right." Tara remembered how there was no such thing as privacy in a small town.

"Too bad. Don't tell Pastor Peabody I said this, but it's my opinion that every town needs a witch." Her expression became thoughtful. "The problem is finding one. Can't hardly advertise in the *Rim Rock Record*."

"I suppose not." Tara could feel her polite smile slipping and was relieved when the cook called Iris back to the kitchen, leaving her to ponder the news that Gavin Thomas had murdered his married lover.

5

After paying her bill — and tacking on a generous tip — she visited her grandmother's attorney to sign the multitude of papers that effectively transferred ownership of the house to her.

"You do understand the conditions of the codicil?" Thatcher Reardon asked, eyeing her over the tortoiseshell frame of his reading glasses.

"That I can't list the house for sale without living in it for a month? Yes."

"Will this be a problem?"

"Not really." Tara sighed. "It's longer than I'd planned to stay away from my business, but I think I can manage. Although I still find it frustrating that my grandmother disapproved so highly of my career choice that she'd pull a stunt like this."

"It wasn't that she disapproved," the sixty-something lawyer said. "On the contrary, she was quite proud of your accomplishments."

"You could have fooled me," Tara muttered.

"If you'd visited her these past two years, perhaps you'd have been in better touch with her feelings."

Although his tone was mild and lacking in censure, Tara prickled at the unspoken accusation. Before the Richard debacle, she'd visited all the time. In fact, she'd even spent most of her childhood summers in Whiskey River. How could she explain that returning to the scene of her greatest embarrassment was too painful?

How, especially, could she make him understand that just being with her grandmother, sensing Brigid's unspoken disappointment at how she'd chosen to turn her back on a family tradition that went back centuries, was too difficult?

She crossed her legs with a swish of silk. Although she knew she was overdressed in her chic black-and-cream suit, she'd wanted to appear businesslike for this meeting. "My grandmother was a wonderful woman, but she could be more than a little intimidating."

"Tell me about it." The lawyer chuckled. "We were bridge partners every Thursday night for ten years and in all that time I never outgrew my fear that she'd turn me into a toad if I misbid."

"A toad?" Tara stared at him. "Are you saying that you knew —"

"That Brigid was a witch?" Thatcher asked easily. "Of course."

"And that didn't bother you?"

He shrugged. "Most people here in Whiskey River tend to have a live-and-let-live attitude. Your grandmother was a warm and generous person, Ms. Delaney. She contributed a great deal to the town and I think there was hardly anyone who didn't show up at her house for help with one thing or another.

"In fact, she gave me some salve that did wonders for my bursitis. And my social life hasn't been the same since she passed." A twinkle brightened his intelligent blue eyes. "Not only was she an excellent cardplayer, but not many eighty-year-old women could do the Texas Two-Step like Brigid Delaney. I suppose it was her theatrical background," he mused out loud.

"My grandmother danced? To country music?"

He looked at her with surprise. "Of course. This is, after all, ranching country."

"Of course," Tara murmured. "Well. That certainly is an interesting piece of news." Wanting to be alone to let it all sink in, she stood and held out her hand. "It was nice meeting you, Mr. Reardon."

"It was nice meeting you, as well, Ms. Delaney. And I'm sure I'll be seeing you around." A significant pause settled over the room, giving Tara the impression that he had not quite finished.

"Was there something else?"

"I was just wondering if you'd considered taking over your grandmother's business."

"No." She picked up her purse and straightened her spine. "I don't do magic, Mr. Reardon. And I don't cast spells."

That said, she left the attorney's office. The next order of business, she'd decided, was a visit with the sheriff.

The office, located on the third floor of the town's eighty-year-old redbrick courthouse, was shabby, but neat. Two mud brown chairs sat in front of a weathered pine desk. A law enforcement recruiting poster featured a scrubbed and polished young man in a starched khaki uniform standing beside a patrol car. Taped to the beige wall next to the poster were crayon drawings, a thank-you from a first-grade class for a tour of the jail.

Trace Callahan was a tall man. Even without the wedge-heeled cowboy boots, Tara would have guessed his height to be around six foot four. His eyes were gunmetal gray, his jaw square, his hair black. He might have traded in a uniform for a plaid shirt and jeans, but even without the silver star pinned to the front of the green-and-black shirt, she would have had no trouble pegging him for a cop. The authority he radiated was a relief; Tara had been worried that the new sheriff might be some burned-out hack who'd ended up in Whiskey River because he couldn't cut it anywhere else.

"Ms. Delaney." His smile was quick and warm, at odds with the harsh lines of his face. "It's good to finally meet you. Brigid talked a great deal about you."

"So I've heard."

"She was very proud of you. And, from what I've heard, with good reason." Sympathy softened the steely color of his eyes. "I'm sorry about your loss. She was a wonderful woman."

"Yes. She was." Tara drew in a determined breath. "I'm not here on a social call, Sheriff Callahan. If you don't mind, I have some questions I'd like to ask you."

"Of course."

Watching him carefully, Tara didn't see a hint of surprise or curiosity. It was his official cop face, she supposed — polite, distant, not giving anything away.

"Would you like some coffee?" he asked easily. "It's fresh."

"No, thank you." She sat down in the chair on the visitor's side of the desk and crossed her legs. "I've had more than enough today." Along with the two cups at the diner, she'd had another at Thatcher Reardon's law office and her nerves were already jangling. The one thing she definitely didn't need was any more caffeine.

The sheriff sat down in the leather chair behind the desk. "I suppose this is about the vandalism to your grandmother's house?"

"Oh, no. That's all been taken care of."

"So Gavin told me. That was clever the way you scared those kids away."

"They didn't really mean any harm. But that's not why I'm here. I wanted to ask you about my grandmother's death."

"What about it?"

"You're certain her heart attack caused her fall?"

His eyes narrowed. So imperceptibly that if Tara hadn't been watching him carefully, she would not have noticed the change. His body had tensed, too, she thought.

"That was the coroner's opinion. Of course, there was also the possibility that her fall caused her to have the heart attack.

The two things were concurrent."

"I see."

There was a little pause.

"Do you have some reason to believe otherwise?"

Tara thought about telling him about her mother's vision, then decided he'd think she was nuts. Which was undoubtedly what he thought about her grandmother.

"Not really."

"I know it's difficult, losing someone you love. But everything pointed to a combination of natural causes and her accident, Ms. Delaney. However, if there's any reason to open the case . . ."

"No." Tara shook her head, wishing she hadn't even brought it up. But now that she was here, there was one other little matter she'd like to clear up. "I do have one more question."

"Shoot."

"What do you know about Gavin Thomas?"

"Ah." He nodded. "You've been talking to Iris."

Tara didn't deny it. "So it's true? He's a convicted murderer?"

"It's not really my place —"

"I don't want to hear it's not your place to tell me, Sheriff," Tara cut him off. "The man managed to befriend my grandmother. Then she died of a so-called accident, and the next thing I know he's staying in her house."

"For the night. To catch the vandals."

"So he says."

"But you don't believe that."

It was not really a question, but Tara answered it, anyway. "I'm not sure."

Trace rubbed his jaw, obviously uncomfortable with the situation. "I can tell you this much," he decided. "Whatever reasons he had for befriending your grandmother had nothing to do with murder. If I believed, for even a minute, that Gavin Thomas was a danger to anyone in Whiskey River, believe me, Ms. Delaney, he wouldn't be running around loose on the streets."

"But even if you thought he was a danger to the community, there really wouldn't be much you could do legally until he slipped up and showed his true colors."

"No offense, Ms. Delaney, but you don't know me. Or what I can do to keep Whiskey River safe."

His jaw had hardened to stone; his eyes were flint. Tara decided she'd gotten about as far as she was going to for one day.

"I'm sorry. I was just distressed to learn that my grandmother had made friends with a convicted murderer."

"He may have been convicted of murder in the second degree," Trace allowed, apparently deciding it was time to set the record straight, "but the conviction was overturned."

"I heard it was overturned on a technicality."

"That's only true if you consider the real killer's confessing to the crime a technicality."

"Is that what happened?"

"That's what happened. And the governor pardoned Gavin. He was the proverbial innocent, framed man, Ms. Delaney. It doesn't happen as often in life as it does in the movies, but it does happen."

"So do false confessions," she couldn't resist pointing out.

"This one was valid."

"You're sure of that."

"I was the investigating detective. I took the statement. Yes, I'm sure."

His no-nonsense voice was edged with cold steel. "Well then, I suppose that's that."

"I suppose it is." His expression, and his voice, softened. "Gavin Thomas made some mistakes, Ms. Delaney. But murder wasn't one of them."

Something about this man and his self-assured manner convinced her. "Thank you, Sheriff." She stood, and held out her hand. "You've no idea how much that relieves me."

"Glad to be of service, Ms. Delaney." He stood, as well, engulfing Tara's hand in one a great deal larger and darker. "May I ask how long you're planning to stay in Whiskey River?"

"I'll be here for the month."

"That long." Trace rubbed his jaw thoughtfully.

"I don't have much choice." She turned to leave. "Goodbye, Sheriff. I suppose I'll be seeing you around."

"I'm sure you will, Ms. Delaney. And once again, I'm sorry about your grandmother."

As Tara left the building, a man sitting on a bench in the small square next to the courthouse rose and followed her at a discreet distance. He wondered what she and the sheriff had been talking about, wondered if she was going to be a problem. If so, she'd have to be dispensed with. He frowned as he thought about Brigid Delaney's untimely accident. If the old woman hadn't been so damn stubborn, she'd still be alive today. That made him wonder if the witch's granddaughter had inherited Brigid's damn intransigence. He hoped, for her sake, that she hadn't.

Perhaps, he considered, mulling over all the possibilities, he could gain her cooperation and save himself a great deal of time. Not that she wouldn't get something out of it, he considered. His lips curved into a cruel, sardonic smile. Like staying alive.

Two hours after her meeting with the sheriff, Tara was back at the house, yanking weeds from the overgrown garden where she'd once waited in vain for Richard to show up for their wedding. It wasn't that she really cared about the garden all that much, she told herself. But it was important for the house and the yard to look its best when she put it up for sale.

"Dammit, Grandy," she muttered as she attacked a dandelion. "It was bad enough making me come back here. Now you've got half the people in town asking if I'm taking over for you. They're probably all waiting for me to turn into a stringy-haired hag with a huge wart on the end of her nose who invokes the winds on alternating Sabbaths."

"Brigid certainly wasn't a hag," a deep, all-too-familiar voice behind her said. "And she didn't have any warts. At least none that I could see."

The voice startled Tara, making her jump. "I didn't hear you drive up." Her expression and her tone were less than welcoming.

"I guess your mind was on something else." Her face was flushed a soft pink hue, whether from sun or embarrassment at having been caught talking to herself, Gavin couldn't tell.

She muttered something that could have been a curse or an agreement, then went back to her weeding with renewed vigor.

When Gavin didn't move, she looked up at him. "Well? Can I do something for you? A little love potion to help you get the woman of your dreams into bed, perhaps? Some magic crystal to bring you fame and fortune? Maybe you'd prefer a tarot reading. Or I could look into my crystal ball and foretell this week's lottery numbers."

She stood and held out her hand. "Cross my palm with silver and I will tell you many, many things about your future."

Her outstretched hand was slim and white, her nails nicely trimmed and unpolished. Ignoring the dirt, he took it in both of his, turning it over to trail a fingertip across the sensitive skin of her palm.

"You have the most incredibly delicate skin." Gavin wondered if she'd be this soft all over and figured she probably would. "You should be extra careful in the sun."

His touch sent a jolt of electricity shooting through the center of her palm straight to her toes, which suddenly curled in her sneakers.

"I put on sunscreen." She tugged her hand loose. "What do you want?" she demanded, her hands splayed on her hips.

His eyes narrowed as they moved in a slow, masculine perusal of her, from the top of her gleaming auburn head down to her feet. She was wearing an oversize cream T-shirt and a pair of faded denim shorts. Her legs were lean and firm and well muscled, revealing that she didn't spend all her time behind a desk.

Although there was nothing remotely seductive about the outfit, Gavin decided she was one of the most appealing women he'd ever seen.

"That's a loaded question. Are you sure you want to know the answer?"

Although she fought against it, Tara found

the seductive glint in his eyes unreasonably compelling.

"Let me put it another way," she amended, determined to avoid the sensual trap he seemed equally determined to lay for her. "What, exactly, are you doing here?"

"Ah." He nodded as he treated her to another of those long, intimate looks that had her breath catching in her suddenly raw throat. "I brought the glass."

"Glass?" She wondered idly if he could be a magician himself. Because the way she was finding it difficult to think about anything but him made her suspect he'd hypnotized her. That was the only logical explanation.

He wondered what she was wearing beneath that oversize shirt. She professed to be a practical, no-nonsense sort of woman, which would suggest white cotton underwear without any frills. But experience had taught him that sometimes the most outwardly sedate females possessed a secret yen for silk and lace.

Either way — silk or cotton — dammit, he wanted her. And had, he realized, from the first moment he'd seen her.

A magic spell?

He almost laughed at the outrageous

idea. How about hormones?

"Did I say something funny?" she asked, annoyed and unreasonably flustered by the humor brightening his eyes.

"No. It's just the circumstances. You and me. And Brigid."

"There isn't any you and me," she insisted. "And there isn't going to be." Her irritation cleared her head. "You mentioned glass. I take it you're here to replace the window."

She'd coated herself in enough ice to encase Jupiter. Gavin was both frustrated by the change and grateful for it. During a long sleepless night, he'd spent too many hours reminding himself that the lady living in Brigid's house offered more complications than he needed. Or wanted.

"I said I would." As if it possessed a mind of its own, his rebellious finger reached out and played with the little wisps of hair curling at the nape of her neck. "You really should put on a hat to shade your face. You're getting burned."

Although he'd only touched her hair, excitement flashed up Tara's rigid spine like chain lightning. She backed up, nearly tripping over the hoe. When he grasped her upper arms to steady her, the feel of those long dark fingers set her blood humming.

Her trembling nerves made her rash. "Don't tell me you've already run out of married women in Whiskey River to seduce?"

"I see the gossip mill has been working overtime."

Shutters had come down over his eyes. The muscle jerking in his dark cheek both frightened and fascinated her.

Tara had regretted her words the minute they'd escaped her mouth. "I'm sorry. I shouldn't have said that. But it's a small town. And you know how people talk."

Wanting to escape the notoriety he'd suffered in Texas, Gavin had hoped that the small, remote western Arizona town would provide a new start. Unfortunately, he'd learned it wasn't all that easy to leave the past behind.

"Would it make a difference if I told you I didn't kill Pamela?"

Pamela. The dead woman now had a name, which made her ever so much more real in Tara's mind. "It doesn't make any difference to me one way or the other," she lied. "Besides, Sheriff Callahan already told me that."

His mouth twisted with bitter amusement at the idea of her interrogating his old buddy. "Been checking up on me,

Tara?" His voice, smooth and sharp at the same time, reminded her of a stiletto swathed in silk.

"You were friends with Brigid. You were also in prison for murder."

"And following that line of thought, since Brigid died unexpectedly, obviously I must have had something to do with it." His expression became speculative. "Maybe you thought I killed her for her collection of crystal balls. Or magic wands."

"I didn't say that."

"You didn't need to. The accusation is written all over your face." And what a face, Gavin thought. He ran the back of his hand down her flushed cheek. "You shouldn't try to lie, Tara. You're really not very good at it."

He was close. Too close. As the vibrations between them hummed through her, Tara forced herself to stay right where she was and not let him see how easily he could unnerve her.

"I'm sorry. It's just that I don't know you, and —"

"We can certainly remedy that."

He rocked forward on the balls of his feet and touched his mouth to hers. The kiss was brief, hard, radiated with lust and was decidedly, frighteningly possessive. A jolt of unfamiliar energy swept through her, and although she'd never felt it before, Tara had no difficulty recognizing it as pure, undiluted passion.

She sucked in a deep breath, hoping the oxygen would stop her head from spinning. "What do you think you're doing?" A distracting mixture of need and fear continued to simmer in her veins.

"Getting to know you." He trailed a treacherous fingertip around her lips. "Letting you get to know me."

"Well, if that was your goal, then you definitely succeeded. And I'm definitely unimpressed." Even as she said the words, Tara braced herself for the bolt of lightning that undoubtedly accompanied such a blatant lie.

"Are you saying you didn't feel anything just now?"

"It was pleasant." She shrugged. "A bit like kissing my brother."

His fingers skimmed around the line of her jaw. "You don't have a brother."

"A favorite cousin, then."

"A cousin." He frowned as he caressed her throat, where the flesh was even silkier than her hand had been. And warmer. "I take it that means no sparks?"

His rough padded fingers created an enervating heat. Though her throat had gone unreasonably dry, Tara managed to speak evenly. "No. No sparks."

Liar. He didn't need to say the words out loud. They hovered between them like a shimmering force field.

"I'd hate to think I was losing my touch. I'd better try again."

She knew it was coming, knew she could stop it. Knew she *should* stop it. But instead, Tara just stood there, looking up at him as he slowly, deliberately lowered his head.

Surprisingly, considering the heat in his gaze, the kiss was gentle. Tender. But the swirl of sultry sensation created by the tip of his tongue encircling her parted lips was devastatingly seductive.

The light touch kindled an instantaneous spark of need. Never, in a million years, could she have imagined the way he could make her entire world spin off its axis with a single kiss. Like the first, it did not last long. Yet during that fleeting time, Tara knew that her life had been forever changed.

"Well." Breathless, she pressed her fingertips to her lips. Tara knew this was the time for a flip, self-assured remark. But it was difficult to think coherently when your mind was reeling.

"Well, indeed."

Hell. He'd intended the kiss to be short and simple. Short it had been. Simple was something else all together. Shaken, but not prepared to admit it, he resisted the urge to haul her back into his arms and kiss her senseless.

"I believe we've just given a whole new meaning to the term 'kissing cousins.' "

"It's only Brigid," Tara insisted shakily. "She's putting thoughts in our minds."

"You can't believe that."

"It's the only logical explanation." Tara could feel her grandmother's spirit looking on, thoroughly enjoying the seductive scenario she'd created.

"Only Brigid's granddaughter would consider a possible haunting to be logical," Gavin said dryly.

He traced her still-tingling lips with his thumb. He wanted her. In all the ways a man could want a woman. He wanted her so damn badly that he could barely breathe from the wanting.

There was something about Tara Delaney, something hot and hidden, like a volcanic river running beneath an ice floe, that he found dangerously appealing. Being a survivor, Gavin knew when to back away.

"Yes, indeed," he drawled, his eyes on

that soft, sweet mouth he could still taste, "it's going to be a very interesting month."

Having thrown down the gauntlet, he released her and headed back to his truck for the window.

She couldn't move, couldn't breathe. Still shaken by what should have been a simple kiss, Tara closed her eyes tight and prayed for calm.

When that didn't work, she grabbed up the hoe and brutally killed another row of weeds.

From his perch on the ladder, Gavin looked out over the garden and watched Tara attacking the tangled undergrowth with a silent fury that suggested she'd rather be swinging that hoe at his head. A familiar knot tightened in his stomach.

Trace was right. It had been too long since he'd enjoyed the little dance of seduction, too long since he'd allowed himself the pleasure of sinking into the fragrant, mindless oblivion of a woman. Too long since he'd gotten laid.

She could insist until that lovely flushed face turned blue that she wasn't interested in taking the chemistry that had sparked between them to its ultimate conclusion.

They both knew she was lying.

Just as they both knew that despite her

words to the contrary, before the thirty days had passed, before any For Sale sign went up on the front lawn, he and Tara Delaney would be lovers.

"Count on it," Gavin murmured as he returned to work, his decision made.

6

Tara was finding sleep an elusive target. Lying alone in the old house was very different from sleeping alone in her modern high-rise apartment. The strange night sounds reminded her of floorboards creaking and doors squeaking open. On several occasions over the past three nights, she'd actually gotten out of bed and gone searching for the source of the noise, thinking that perhaps a cat, or some other animal, had gotten into the house. But each time she couldn't find anything, she'd assured herself that the mysterious sounds were nothing more than a century-old house settling down for the night.

Unfortunately, telling herself that and believing it were two different things. And when she did drift off, dreams of Gavin proved anything but restful. The hot, sensual dreams had her tossing and turning and waking up exhausted and needy.

She told herself that she should feel relieved that there'd been no sign of him. Instead, his disappearing act had her growing more and more tense.

"He's obviously wanting me to wonder what he's up to," she muttered to herself as she braved the task of cleaning her grandmother's cluttered study. "Or perhaps he's already changed his mind about wanting to seduce me."

Not that there was any chance of his succeeding, Tara assured herself. But even as she told herself she wasn't the least bit interested, she had to admit she was irked by the idea that he'd lose interest so quickly.

Brigid had definitely been a hoarder; Tara doubted her grandmother had thrown anything away during her eight decades on earth. Myriad texts climbed up the forest green wainscotted walls on creamy white shelves, were stacked atop tables, tumbled over the cushions of velvet-covered wing chairs and nearly covered the faded carpet.

Crystals — glittering gifts from the earth possessed with an inner energy waiting to be liberated — were everywhere. Her first day in the house, Tara had washed all the windows; now a gold-tinged autumn sun streamed through the sparkling glass. The warm morning rays struck a large piece of quartz on the ornately carved mahogany partner's desk, and the room took on a rosy glow as Tara set to work cataloging all the books.

Since she had fond memories of many of the books of Celtic myths her grandmother had read to her when she was a child, Tara decided to take them back to San Francisco with her, never mind the fact that her apartment was already overflowing with business and investment texts.

Those books dealing with druid ceremonies and beliefs she'd ship to her mother. The rest — novels embracing every genre of fiction from fantasy to horror to romance — she decided to donate to the Rim Country Rescue Unit, a volunteer group providing 911 emergency service to the remote mountain communities. She'd unearthed a letter on her grandmother's desk from the organization requesting donated items for a tag sale planned for Halloween weekend. The handwritten note in the margin revealed that Brigid had intended to contribute signed copies of her books.

Having woken up edgy, this trip down memory lane only made Tara more tense. Her mood wasn't helped by the knowledge that something was coming. She could sense it in every atom of her body.

"So long as it isn't *someone*," she muttered as she moved a Ouija board off a green marble-topped table to make room for a gloriously illustrated book of fairy tales that had so enthralled her as a child. *Someone like Gavin Thomas.* She glanced out the window, half expecting to see the cause of all her uncharacteristic anxiety striding up the front walk. When she didn't, she told herself that she was really beginning to lose her mind.

Frustrated, she returned to work with a renewed vengeance. The thing to do, she told herself, was to keep so busy that she didn't have time to think of Gavin. Or her life.

The task did not go swiftly. She kept running across personal belongings that stirred bittersweet memories. A lodestone on which a love rune had been scratched vibrated in her palm, reminding Tara that Brigid had professed to have been carrying this very stone in the pocket of her dress the night she'd met Jared Brown, the man who had become Tara's grandfather. Soothed by the fact that the stone still carried Brigid's life force within it, Tara slipped it into the pocket of her jeans.

A silver chalice, etched with ancient symbols, claimed the top of a lace-draped marble-topped table. Hanging on the wall behind the table was an ornate gold sword encrusted with semiprecious stones.

Candles of all sizes, shapes and colors adorned the top of the old upright piano where, as a little girl, Tara had practiced her scales and learned to play two-handed "Chopsticks." Scattered atop nearby tables were decks of tarot cards, clay potpourri pots and small, hand-painted wooden boxes. Inside a box adorned with decoupage pictures of the galaxies, Tara found a pair of earrings she remembered well. And a small piece of obsidian on a thin silver chain she'd never seen before.

Although the dangling silver crescent moons were far more flamboyant than the small pearl studs she usually wore to work, Tara slipped them on and felt an instant sense of connection with her grandmother that comforted and saddened her at the same time. She slipped the necklace over her head and tucked it beneath her sweater where it warmed her skin.

In a drawer of an antique rolltop desk, alleged to have once belonged to that master illusionist Houdini, she discovered a stack of letters requesting her grandmother's appearance as a featured speaker at various druid gatherings. Deciding that good manners required her to respond, she'd just put them aside to deal with later when, beneath the letters, she unearthed a book that captured her immediate attention.

The cover featured a drawing of an impossibly voluptuous, barely clad woman flying through a sea of twinkling stars seated astride a silver-handled broom. Only the fact that the book was hardcover and an outrageous price suggested that it was not a mere comic book.

Morganna, Mistress of the Night? She read the title out loud. "What on earth would Grandy be doing with something like this?"

The only possible explanation was that Brigid had been preparing an article attacking such a piece of slanderous trash. Instead of the typical ugly old crone of fairy tales, this witch was the other side of the coin, a side that was every bit as untruthful and unflattering — the evil temptress.

A cold fury flowed through Tara as she skimmed through the pages depicting the female witch conducting various so-called rituals. Most of the rituals, Tara noticed, involved Morganna shedding her clothes beneath a bloodred or, in some instances, a milk white moon. Although her free-flowing ebony hair managed — just barely — to cover her breasts and the shadowy juncture between her thighs, the luscious enchantress had a body any *Playboy* centerfold would envy.

The magic conducted within the sacred circle was stereotypical black sorcery involving bubbling cauldrons, black cats and bats. It also, Tara noted, was more often than not used as a tool of vengeance.

Shaking her head with disdain and disgust, Tara was about to throw the book into the trash when an inscription on the inside title page captured her attention.

The script was bold and dark, suggesting a very strong masculinity. The powerful vibrations emanating from it were palpable.

"To Brigid — with affection and admiration," Tara read. Her eyes narrowed at the next line. "Gavin Thomas?"

How dare he! What made him think he could attack everything her grandmother believed in with such impunity? And then to have the absolute gall to rub a dear, elderly woman's nose in such unmitigated filth was purely unconscionable!

Tara threw the book into the wastebasket. Then plucked it out again. She was intending to burn it to cinders in the fireplace when the doorbell chimed. Unfortunately, she knew instantly who'd come calling.

She stomped to the door and flung it open. "You have a lot of nerve!"

The first thought that flashed through Gavin's mind was that he hadn't imagined Tara Delaney's beauty. She was, in a word, stunning. She was also furious. Although he'd never experienced anything resembling a psychic moment in his life — he refused to consider the hot dreams he'd been having the past three nights to be any type of omen — he certainly didn't need second sight to envision the flames encircling her bright head. Flames that were a distinct contrast to the frost in her sharp gaze.

Fire and ice. Gavin had always been a man to appreciate contradictions.

"Good morning to you, too." There was both amusement and annoyance in his deep voice. "I was driving into town and thought I'd stop by and see if you needed anything."

Tara's icy gaze raked over him. "Go to hell."

She slammed the door, but with the deftness of an aluminum-siding salesman, Gavin slipped his foot between the door and the jamb, preventing her from shutting him out. "That's a bit longer trip than I had in mind."

"Tough." She pushed harder, frustrated

when the thick oak door refused to budge.

"Can I take your lack of hospitality to mean that you're not a morning person?"

"If you don't leave right this minute, I'll call the sheriff and have him arrest you for trespassing."

"Don't you think that's overreacting just a bit?"

She made a low sound of fury. "After what you've done, you're lucky I don't turn you into a toad!"

Lord, the lady was passionate beneath that cool exterior! It made Gavin want to push a few more buttons just to see how fast and how hot she'd heat up.

"Good try. But you'll find I'm not as easily terrified as those kids the other night. Who, by the way, have arranged to make restitution for your window."

She was momentarily sidetracked. "How do you know that?"

"I played poker with the sheriff last night. He told me."

"It would have been nice if he'd told me."

"If you'd been down at the jail playing five card stud with us, I imagine he would have. I expect he'll be calling you later today."

"How considerate of him. I suppose I

should be grateful that he's not going to make me wait and read the news in the *Rim Rock Record*."

"You know, Tara, sarcasm doesn't really suit you." When he reached out and lightly brushed those tantalizing wisps of bright hair at the back of her neck, she took a quick step back, realizing too late that she'd just allowed him entry into her house.

"Go away."

"You know, if you're not careful, I'm going to think you don't like me."

"And you'd be right. Tell me one reason why I shouldn't boil in oil the horrid person who wrote this." She jammed the hateful book into his stomach.

"Ah." Ignoring the fact that she'd nearly knocked the wind out of him, Gavin began flipping through the pages, much as she had done. There was the faintest of smiles around his mouth. "I take it you're underwhelmed."

Tara backed farther away and crossed her arms over the front of her oversize emerald green sweater. "Since we first met, I've tried to figure out what it was that my grandmother liked about you," she said between clenched teeth. "But despite my best efforts, whatever charms you may possess continue to escape me."

116

"That's undoubtedly because you haven't taken the time to get to know me."

"You haven't exactly given me the opportunity." The words were no sooner out of her mouth when she realized she'd made a grave tactical error by revealing she'd been aware of his absence.

"If I'd known you missed me, I would have visited again a lot sooner." Staying away had been the hardest thing he'd ever done, harder than eighteen months in a Texas state penitentiary, Gavin thought with grim humor.

"I'd rather be visited by plague and pestilence."

Fire flashed in her remarkable eyes, glowed hotly in her cheeks. She was, Gavin thought again, a woman of amazing passions.

"Do you always smell so good?" he asked, suddenly changing the subject to what was uppermost in his mind at the moment. "And you have the most fascinating skin. It looks like cool, perfectly smooth porcelain, but it feels like silk that's been lying beneath a buttery summer sun."

"Dammit, Gavin —"

"It makes a man wonder," he continued, huskily overriding her faint protest, "if the rest of your body is as soft. As warm."

"Don't touch me." Determined to regain some control of the situation, she knocked his hand away when he began to toy with a dangling silver earring. "And don't talk to me that way."

"How would you like me to talk to you?"

"I'd like you to say goodbye."

"Not until you agree to come for a ride with me." Ignoring her instructions not to touch, he took her hand, lacing their fingers together. "There's something I want to show you."

"I've already seen your etchings, remember?" She tried to pull her hand free, but was forestalled when he tightened his grip. He wasn't hurting her, but the increased force succeeded in holding her captive. "There's no way I'm going anywhere with you."

"Surely you're not that afraid of me?"

"I'm not afraid at all," she said, not quite truthfully. While she was no longer worried he was a murderer, there was nothing comforting about the way he made her feel. "I told you, I just don't like you."

"Are you always tempted to go to bed with men you don't like?"

"You're a very lucky man," she said between clenched teeth. "Because I am managing, just barely, to keep from slapping you for that remark, clichéd though that response may be."

"It's the truth. And we both know it. You may not want me to want you. Hell, *I* don't want to want you. But I don't seem to have a lot of choice in the matter. And neither do you. So —" he shrugged "— the way I see it, we may as well relax and go with the flow."

"I'm not going anywhere with you," she repeated. "And I'm definitely not a believer in going with the flow."

"That's probably why you decided to become an accountant," he considered.

"My reasons for whatever I do, including my career choice, are none of your business. Besides," she said, belatedly remembering what had so angered her in the first place, "I've already planned to spend the day cleaning the clutter out of my grandmother's house."

She glared down at the book in his hand. "Beginning with that piece of trash. After having seen it, I'm forced to wonder just how much you had to do with her heart attack."

The blow was swift, sharp and direct. And surprisingly painful.

"Bull's-eye," he murmured. "You have

very good aim, sweetheart. Nearly as good as Morganna's when she took on those muggers in Central Park."

Tara tossed up her chin. "You can't possibly be comparing me with your underdressed, oversexed cartoon character?"

"If the cat suit fits," he murmured. He treated her to another one of those slow, head-to-toe appraisals that gave her the impression he was imagining her in a clinging black body stocking. "And yes, although you might not be as voluptuous as my mistress of the night, I'd say there's a definite resemblance."

"You are not only obnoxious, you're crazy."

"That's pretty much the same thing Brigid said the first time she met my fictional witch," he allowed. "But she gradually began to appreciate certain aspects of Morganna's nature. Enough so that she was willing to provide a great deal of input in later editions."

"You're lying. My grandmother spent her entire life striving to overcome negative stereotypes like your ridiculous comic book and I refuse —"

"Graphic novel."

She waved off his correction with a furious gesture. "I refuse," she began again, "to believe she would have anything to do with you. Or your comic creation."

"Graphic novel," he repeated again.

"There's no difference."

"Of course there is." Although his tone remained mild, the glint in his midnight-dark eyes reminded her that, although he might not be a cold-blooded murderer, Gavin was nevertheless dangerous.

"Come for a drive with me and I'll prove your grandmother really was a friend. And a fan."

Impossible. There was absolutely nothing he could do to convince Tara that her grandmother had approved of such trash.

Still, no one had ever accused Brigid Delaney of being predictable. And some of the things Gavin had said about Brigid suggested, as impossible as it was to imagine, that they'd been close.

"I have a meeting with the Realtor who's going to list the house this afternoon at two."

"I'll get you back in plenty of time. Don't you think it's what Brigid would want you to do?"

That was definitely dirty pool. Especially since Tara secretly admitted he was right. She let out a long sigh of reluctant surrender. "This I have to hear."

As he walked beside her to his fire engine red Chevy Tahoe parked outside the house, Gavin managed, just barely, to restrain his triumphant smile.

7

Tara was not surprised when Gavin drove fast. Faster than the law allowed, faster than what would be, for most people, a prudent speed over the rough red cinders. However, as much as she hated to admit it, as he deftly swerved around a huge rock that was taking up the center of the road, in this case, his irritating self-confidence seemed warranted.

"I still can't believe you could know my grandmother and write that disgusting comic book," she said when he barely slowed down at a four-way stop on the deserted stretch of road.

"Graphic novel. And for the record, I hadn't met your grandmother when I came up with the idea for Morganna."

"But you're still writing comic — graphic novels," she quickly corrected herself, determined not to become sidetracked by technicalities. She wanted to argue the content of his work, not the name by which it was called.

"I'm like everyone else. I have to pay the rent."

"By causing emotional pain to others, including an elderly woman who befriended you? And what about giving young boys skewed stereotypes of women? Surely you can't be proud of that."

Gavin sighed. "Tara, my books are entertainment. Nothing more, nothing less."

"Entertainment for men." Like strip joints and massage parlors, she tacked on mentally.

"Granted, they're geared to a male audience. And sure, a lot of that audience is possibly under the age of consent, but believe me, teenagers today get a lot more sex, violence and skewed stereotypes on television. Have you watched those MTV videos?"

"So what you're saying is, that since such harmful, chauvinistic attitudes are so prevalent in society, you have absolutely no compunction about ducking responsibility for creating outrageous sexual stereotypes for profit."

"Ouch." He flinched and shook his head. "I guess I'll just have to change your mind about Morganna."

"That won't happen."

"Never say never."

Gavin turned the truck onto something that seemed more rocky creek bed than proper road, and Tara hung on to the handle above the passenger door as the Tahoe bounced across the boulder-strewn road.

Still troubled by the thought of how painful her grandmother would have found Gavin's portrayal of witches, she said suddenly, "You didn't really believe Brigid was a witch, did you?"

After meeting Brigid Delaney, and listening to her calm explanation of the craft, Gavin had given a great deal of thought to the matter and had come to the conclusion that she was a nice, albeit slightly delusional old lady. She might even be on the right track with that herbal healing stuff. After all, hadn't a lot of today's modern pharmaceuticals originally come from herbs and bark?

But a witch?

No way.

"No offense, sweetheart," he said as he pulled up in front of a small but cozy-looking log cabin, "but the entire idea is a bit of a stretch. Even for a man with my vivid imagination and active fantasy life."

The look he gave her suggested exactly how vivid. And how active.

"I didn't come here to discuss your fantasy life."

"Too bad," he drawled as he pulled the keys from the ignition and pocketed them. "Because believe me, ever since you showed up at Brigid's house in the middle of that thunderstorm, they've definitely gotten interesting.

"In fact, there's this one really hot one, where I've built a fire in the forest and you appear, looking like every red-blooded male's midnight fantasy, in this long, clinging white satin nightgown, with lace so delicate it looks as if it could have been spun by magic spiders, and —"

"You don't have to tell me any more, Gavin. I get the drift."

"I rather thought you would," he said in a way that told her that, although it made no logical sense, he suspected she'd been experiencing the same sensual dream. Which she had, dammit.

It was all Brigid's doing, Tara told herself. That's all it could be. That's all she would allow it to be.

Gavin's cabin was compact. And cluttered. Papers appeared to cover every flat surface, including the maple dining room table, suggesting he sketched while he ate. Filing cabinets and bookshelves lined the knotty-pine walls. On a shelf beside the door, she noticed a blue bottle filled

126

with soil and sealed with wax.

"Is that from my grandmother?"

Gavin followed her gaze. "Brigid gave it to me when I first moved in. She promised it would protect my home. Unfortunately, she didn't have any charmed dirt that would also keep it neat.

"Make yourself at home," he invited, gathering up a pile of newspapers from a plaid sofa that had seen better days. "I'll make some coffee. Unless you'd rather have tea. I think I have some herbal tea bags that Brigid gave me."

"Coffee's fine."

He left the room. A moment later Tara heard the sounds of drawers opening and water running.

She wove her way through the clutter, past the weight machine and the slanted drafting table toward the couch, stepping over the piles of papers that were arranged in a way that led her to suspect that he might actually have a system of sorts. Needless to say, it was a far cry from her own tidy files and ledgers.

She paused at a bookshelf filled with texts about witchcraft. Some she knew were well written, carefully researched, accurate portrayals of the craft. Others were nothing more than myth and false legends, penned by charlatans who were only interested in making a quick buck. Which was, she reminded herself, exactly what Gavin was guilty of doing.

"Interesting library you've collected," she said when he returned.

"Brigid was a bit more blunt the first time she visited. She returned the next day with armloads of books she insisted I read."

"And did you?"

"Of course. And although I realize it will burst your little bubble of disapproval, I actually took some of the writings to heart."

She sat down on the couch and crossed her legs. "How generous of you."

Her scathing tone only made him laugh. "You're a hard nut to crack, Tara. For someone who's turned her back on her heredity."

"How did you know about that?"

"I told you, Brigid was a friend of mine. We shared a lot. I told her about my life growing up in Dallas, and she told me all about her family."

He handed her an earthenware mug and sat down beside her, so close their thighs were touching. Since she did not want him to know how unnerving she found the feel of his leg against hers, she refrained from scooting over.

Tara took a sip of the coffee. It was dark and rich and had a faint taste of vanilla. "This is very good."

"You don't have to sound so surprised. Despite the admittedly less than domestic atmosphere around here, I know my way around a kitchen."

"I imagine I could count on one hand the number of men I know who could say that."

"It's no big deal. I learned out of self-defense when I figured out that even a kid couldn't live on mayo sandwiches alone."

"Your parents didn't cook?"

"My mother had to work three jobs to keep the wolf away from the door," he revealed. "My father was away most of the time."

"Was he a traveling salesman?"

So, he thought, the Whiskey River gossip mill didn't know his whole life history, just the past few years. "Actually, he was a thief."

"A thief?" She stared at him. "You're making that up." He didn't immediately answer. But there was no need. She could read the truth in his mind, as clearly as it had been printed in the headline of the

Dallas Times Herald. "He robbed banks," she murmured, as much to herself as to Gavin.

Shock radiated through him like waves of energy after an earthquake. "How the hell did you know that?" He knew she hadn't been in contact with her grandmother for two years. And the only other two people, besides Brigid, who knew about his rocky past were Trace and Mariah.

"I'm afraid I read your mind," she said apologetically. "I truly am sorry. I was brought up not to pry into people's thoughts, and I never have before, but this time it just happened."

He gave her a long, hard look. Then reminded himself that Brigid herself had displayed unnerving psychic tendencies. Not that such abilities had made her a witch, Gavin reminded himself.

"Perhaps the fact that so much of Brigid's energy is still lingering in her house has intensified your emotions, so you don't have as much self-control."

"You felt it, too?"

"It would have been hard not to."

She considered his admission and realized that, although he himself didn't know it, Gavin was more of a believer than he thought. "Tell me about him."

"Who?"

"Your father."

Gavin shrugged. "There's not that much to tell. Some men go to banks to work — Pop's chosen career was to rob them. Kinda like Jesse James. But unlike old Jesse, he wasn't very good at it, so he tended to get caught. The fourth time, the judge tossed him into prison and threw away the key."

"So he's still in prison?"

"He died. In a prison riot when I was a teenager. He wasn't one of the instigators. Actually, as strange as it may sound, Pops was a pretty passive, easygoing guy. His death was just a case of being in the wrong place at the wrong time."

"I'm sorry."

He glanced down at her hand on his arm. He'd wanted her to touch him. But not in pity. "It wasn't that big a deal. I hardly knew him. I was born during his second incarceration. He was only home about a year and a half when I was six. Then, when I was fifteen, he lasted three months on parole before he screwed up again."

Gavin didn't add that having been an unwilling guest at the juvenile detention

131

center himself at the time, he'd missed that occasion. It was there he'd met Trace, who was doing his own stint behind bars for being foolish — or unlucky — enough to be driving the car when the kids he was with had decided not to pay for the beer they'd picked up at a convenience store.

Although she knew he didn't want her sympathy, Tara couldn't keep her emotions from showing in her eyes as she looked into his face, for the first time seeing a depth she'd purposefully overlooked earlier.

"That must have been difficult for you." She thought about her own life growing up on the farm, running free, exulting in the glory of nature. Then she remembered how badly she'd wanted to escape such a halcyon existence and live in the big city where no one knew who she was. Or more importantly, *what* she was.

"I think," Gavin said slowly, honestly, "it was harder on my mom, struggling so hard and being alone. She died shortly after she got the news about my dad getting shot in prison. I think she just gave up."

"What happened to you?"

Gavin frowned as he took a long drink of coffee. "As you can see, I survived nicely. And I didn't bring you here to talk about my childhood."

He put his cup down on the pine table in front of the couch, stood and walked over to a cluttered desk.

"Here are the two books I wrote after I met your grandmother," he said, placing them beside her. "Read them and let me know what you think. And since it drives me nuts watching anyone read my stuff, I'm going outside."

Which he did. A moment later, Tara heard the thud of an ax hitting wood.

Unbidden, looking like some ragged-edged old photo, a picture swirled before her eyes — an image of Gavin chopping wood behind the cabin.

The image came to life, allowing her to witness the way he raised the ax over his head and brought it down with a smooth male grace that suggested he was no novice at physical labor. She could hear the thud of the ax against the gnarled alligator bark, smell the pungent sweet scent of juniper berries, feel the Indian summer sun that was warming the scene and turning it a gleaming amber gold.

Wiping his sweaty brow with the back of his hand, he shrugged out of his jacket and threw it casually atop the pile of wood he'd already stacked. A moment later, the white T-shirt followed, revealing that same rock-

133

hard dark chest that had haunted her dreams. Entranced, she watched the rippling of those long muscles in his back, flexing and releasing, again and again, as he proceeded to split the logs into kindling.

Determined to fight the deep sensual pull the vision evoked, Tara turned her attention to the books Gavin had given her to read.

What the hell was she doing in there? Gavin wondered. Reading the words out loud one at a time? He couldn't remember ever being so nervous. Not even when he'd been called before that grim-faced Dallas juvenile judge. Or later, when he'd waited to find out if his parole officer was going to sign the scholarship papers for that fancy arts college that was a long way from the welding or air-conditioning school most of the county's juvenile delinquents were funneled into.

He hadn't even been this uptight waiting for his first Morganna story to sell. And he'd been behind bars at the time.

Although it shouldn't really matter what Tara Delaney thought, Gavin discovered that it did. A lot. Frustrated by this strange new insecurity, he renewed his attack on the wood.

After finishing her second reading of

both books, Tara went outside to locate Gavin. Although the sky had clouded over, the day was still unseasonably warm. He had taken his shirt off and he looked just as she'd pictured him, tan flesh stretched over sinew and muscle, rippling as he continued to chop the wood. He was her vision come to life. Struggling to control her heartbeat, she walked toward him.

With his back turned to her, Gavin was unaware of her approach. When he continued to hack away at the wood as if he held some personal grudge against the logs, Tara cleared her throat. When that failed to gain his attention, she reached out and touched his shoulder.

"Excuse me."

Her light touch was like a brand, scorching his flesh and making him miss the stump on the downswing. He spun toward her.

"Don't you know any better than to sneak up on a man wielding an ax?"

"I'm sorry. But I certainly wasn't trying to sneak up on you."

He could smell her over his own sweat. Her scent was spicy and delicious. And so tempting it made his stomach tighten. He lifted the ax again and embedded it in the top of the stump, then shoved his hands deep into his pockets. "I apologize for yelling at you. My mind was wandering."

"I imagine chopping wood is conducive to thinking through plots."

He liked the fact that she understood. "That's usually the case. But I wasn't thinking about Morganna this time."

Warning signals flashed. Tara chose to heed them and ignored his remark. "You put my grandmother in your novel."

She hadn't called it a comic book, Gavin noted. Things were beginning to look up. "The wise woman of Misty Mountain," he agreed with a nod. "Morganna's spiritual adviser."

"Who reminds Morganna about the Rule of Three when she wants to embark on a crusade of blood and fire against the undead spirits of the moon who have infiltrated the bodies of humans."

" 'Ever mind the Rule of Three,' " Gavin quoted. " 'Three times what thou givest, returns to thee.' " The admonition stressed that any witch who chose to use her powers for evil would ultimately find that evil turning back on her.

"Yet, even after learning the Rule of Three, Morganna doesn't abandon her plans for revenge."

Gavin shrugged. "She's like all of us,

witch or human. She has a dark side and a light side. Life is little more than striving for balance between the two."

This also was exactly what her grandmother had taught her. "Did you learn that from Brigid?"

"No." His wry smile seemed to be directed inward. "That lesson comes from personal experience."

There were things he wasn't telling her. Tara wondered how much of that experience — including his time in prison — was responsible for his having created such an angry, vengeful character.

"I like Brianna," she said.

"Ah." He smiled. "Morganna's twin sister. The virgin witch."

Tara arched a tawny brow. "I don't believe I recall reading that she was a virgin."

"It's implied. Her mind, heart and soul are so unrelentingly pure, it's obvious she'd never succumb to something as primal and dangerous as lust. Speaking of which . . ."

Tara tried to move away, but when her back ran into the trunk of a spreading oak tree, he put both hands on either side of her head, palms against tree, effectively holding her captive. The air around them had become strangely still and the light was that peculiar yellow hue that suggested an impending change in the weather.

"Gavin . . ."

"I like the way you say my name. With that little hitch in your voice." His voice was rough. His dark eyes, looking at her with such unmasked desire, were more potent that a hundred words of seduction. "Say it again."

There was a storm brewing. She could feel it. In the air. Inside her. One thing Tara had never been able to resist was a storm. "Gavin . . ."

"Lord, that's sweet." He leaned closer. Even if he'd wanted to, he could not have prevented his gaze from lingering on her mouth. "I think I was wrong."

"About what?" she managed through lips that had gone impossibly dry. She was trembling. Aching. Waiting.

"About there being no such thing as witchcraft." His lips were a few scant inches from hers, his warm breath stirring smoldering embers. "Because believe me, darlin' —" confident she would not bolt, he ran the back of his fingers down the side of her face "— you definitely have me bewitched."

His mouth brushed against hers, then retreated. "Bothered." Again his lips touched hers. "Bewildered."

The hand that had been creating sparks on her cheek streaked upward and fisted in her hair. The boiling pewter clouds overhead had darkened to deep purple. "I've wanted you since you first collapsed at my feet during that thunderstorm. You've haunted my dreams. And now, dammit, you're haunting me when I'm awake."

His eyes were hot and frustrated. Hers were wary and serious.

"Although I haven't wanted to, I've been thinking of you, too," Tara admitted breathlessly. "Too much. Which, I suppose, makes us even."

"No." Anger flashed, like sheet lightning threatening on the horizon. "Not hardly. Not yet."

8

The storm broke, hot and heavy. Gavin's mouth took hers with none of the sophisticated seduction Tara was accustomed to from the men she dated, men who inhabited her world of white shirts, dark ties and business journals. He did not draw her slowly into the mist, but dragged her instantly into the raging, speeding winds and black sky of the hurricane.

Tara didn't feel the rough tree bark against her back, only the unforgiving strength of his hard male body against hers. She heard the low rumble of thunder and had no idea whether it was coming from the sky or from inside her.

She felt the rushing and swirling of the four winds, stronger than any called up by any mythic sorcerer. Although it was not yet noon, she had the feeling of racing through the night. She kissed him back, hotly, hungrily, without inhibitions, without restraint.

Together they were caught up in the tempest. Lightning flashed as his mouth burned over hers, his teeth nipping at her parted lips, his tongue diving deep.

Using only his wicked, wonderful mouth, he shattered her delicate defenses like a gale force wind shatters glass. Tara had kept her emotions rigorously under control for years. Now recklessness, too long restrained, broke free. She heard a moan as his lips skimmed down her neck and realized the low, desperate sound had escaped her own ravaged lips.

Take me, it said. *Here. Now.*

Gavin thrust his hands beneath her sweater, and through the thin barrier of silk covering her breasts he felt her warm flesh. He could feel the wild beat of her heart pounding beneath his hand, he could taste it throbbing in her throat.

Images swirled in his mind, visions of Tara standing in the streaming silvery glow of moonshine, wearing nothing but that evocative scent of night-blooming flowers, the light of desire shining in her star-bright eyes.

That was followed by another provocative image of the two of them, rolling naked in the wildflower-strewn meadow behind her grandmother's house, lips fused, limbs entwined, sun-warmed flesh gleaming in the clear mountain light.

Fired by the sensual mental pictures, Gavin returned his mouth to hers to plunder and savage. His hands tightened on her breasts, causing a muffled cry to escape her ravaged lips. The sound managed to make its way through the thunderous roaring in his head, capturing his unwilling attention.

It cost Gavin dearly to draw back, but somehow he did. The first thing he noticed as he struggled for breath was that Tara was no longer trembling. But he was.

She was an enchantress. Circe. Lorelie. Morgan Le Fay. She was Brigit, Celtic goddess of fire. She was all the goddesses of all the myths rolled up into one delectable, irresistible package.

She was also the most dangerous female he'd ever met.

And for a man who'd ended up in prison for bedding the wrong woman, that was definitely saying something.

The memories of that wild, out-of-control time were not the least bit pleasant. He shoved them back where they belonged, into the dark corner of his brain that was filled with lessons learned the hard way.

"Although I usually like to finish what I begin," he said in a voice roughened with lingering need, "I promised to get you back home in time for your meeting with that Realtor."

The momentary blank look on her face told him that she'd forgotten all about that. Which meant that she'd been every bit as shaken by that kiss as he. When those wide, slightly unfocused eyes stirred something inside him that was much more than sexual need. Gavin reminded himself that while she might not be as treacherous and self-serving as Pamela Carrington had been, this gorgeous, sweet-smelling female was still trouble. With a capital *T*.

As if some demented part of him was determined to touch his hand to the flames yet again, he heard himself saying, "Have dinner with me. We'll pick up where we left off."

"I don't think that's a good idea."

"Give me one reason why not." Gavin could easily name a dozen right off the top of his head. Including the vow he'd taken to never again allow any woman to become important enough to hurt him. But at the moment, with her taste still on his lips and her scent filling his mind, none of them seemed to matter.

Tara reminded herself that Gavin was a dangerous man. He wasn't the kind of man a woman feared, but the kind a woman would desire. And that, she warned herself, could lead her straight into treacherous waters.

"How about because I don't know what you want from me?"

"Of course you do." His eyes darkened as they roamed over her face, taking in the confusion and reluctant desire in her eyes, the high color in her cheeks. "I want you, Tara. In all the ways a man can want a woman. I have from the beginning. I want to make love to you, to take you places you've never been, to take us both to places we've only dreamed of."

"Well." She let out a long breath. "That's certainly specific."

"I've never been much on game playing." Which was, he'd realized later, exactly why Pamela had chosen him as a pawn in her deadly little game in the first place.

All too aware of how Gavin had maneuvered her into this situation, Tara was tempted to argue that point, but was afraid she'd get sidetracked. "All right, so now I know what you want. But it's not that simple."

"Of course it is." He brushed his thumb over her lips, rewarded when they parted ever so slightly.

She backed away again. "The thing is, Gavin, I don't know what *I* want."

"Maybe not now," he allowed. "But we both know exactly what you wanted when I kissed you. When you kissed me back."

"Your point." She dragged a shaky hand through her hair. "But that was then. And this is now. And despite my grandmother's penchant for serendipity, I've never been a spontaneous person. Sex is distracting. I need time to think."

"Terrific. You'll have all the time you need. Before I pick you up at seven for dinner."

He was doing it again! Steamrollering over her wishes, ignoring her protests. Tara decided that whatever happened between the two of them in the next twenty-seven days, it was important that she set down some ground rules.

"All right. Since I get the feeling you're not going to give up, I'll have dinner with you." She watched the spark of masculine satisfaction in his eyes and knew she was right not to make this easy. "*Tomorrow* night."

It definitely wasn't his first choice. He suspected if he pushed he could win her over, but that wasn't what he wanted. When she came to him — and Gavin pos-

145

sessed not a single doubt that she would —
he wanted her to be in his bed of her own
free will.

Giving her time to think about that hot
kiss, letting her anticipate their lovemaking, was probably not a bad idea.

"You've got yourself a date," he said.

As they walked back toward the house,
Gavin considered that Tara was definitely
turning out to be a challenge. Brigid's
granddaughter smelled like heaven, tasted
like honey warmed by a benevolent sun
and intrigued him like no other mortal
woman ever had.

In fact, now that he thought about it, the
only other female he'd ever met who had
the ability to fascinate him on so many different levels was Morganna, Mistress of
the Night.

Oh, yes, Gavin thought, the next few
weeks were going to be very interesting.

Neither spoke on the way back to
Brigid's house. But the silence was surprisingly companionable. Gavin liked a woman
who didn't feel the need to fill in those inevitable silences with conversation.

He pulled up in front of the house at the
same time a car arrived from the opposite
direction. A metallic sign on the front door
advertised Rim Rock Realty.

"Thank you for the enlightening morning," Tara said.

"It was my pleasure. Wait a minute," he said as she reached for the door handle, prepared to make her escape. "I forgot something."

She glanced back at him over her shoulder. "What now?"

"This." He caught her uplifted chin between his thumb and index finger and touched his mouth to hers.

The chemistry between them was the same as it had been the other times they'd shared a kiss: instant heat, instant need. His mouth, as it devoured hers, was hard and greedy. Tara's blood heated, her skin tingled. Underlying the unbelievably powerful kiss was a faint threat of violence that knocked the breath out of her and made her chest ache.

Forgetting all about the woman who'd gotten out of the car and was walking toward them, forgetting everything but this powerful, painful need ripping through her, Tara opened to him, mouth, mind and heart.

As her body pressed anxiously against his, as he somehow heard her soft little moans over the roaring in his head, Gavin had a vision of dragging her into the back of the Tahoe, stripping her clothes off her, then pounding into her, deep and hard in a mindless melding of flesh, dragging her into the heat and flames until she screamed. And then he'd take her up all over again. And again.

It was her breathy voice, gasping his name that brought him back to reality. Cursing, he took his hand from beneath her sweater and forced himself to relinquish the glory of that lush feminine mouth.

"You're going to kill me yet, sweetheart."

His forehead was pressed against hers, his breath was harsh and labored. Tara could hardly breathe herself.

"This is insane," she managed.

He lifted his head and looked down into her eyes, which were dark and cautious. "You're probably right," he surprised her by agreeing. "But it's still something we're going to have to deal with."

She sighed. "Yes."

She looked so small, so vulnerable, that Gavin found his heart going out to her. Dammit, he didn't want to care for her, didn't want to care *about* her. Understanding that this uncharacteristic feeling of tenderness was even more dangerous than the hunger that had been tormenting him for days, he decided that it was past time to back away.

"We've got company."

She glanced out the windshield and saw the middle-aged woman standing on the sidewalk, studiously looking toward the house, trying to pretend she hadn't witnessed what was going on inside the truck.

"I'll bet she can't wait to get back to town with this little story." Tara groaned. "What am I going to say?"

Her plaintive tone made Gavin chuckle. "Tell her the truth."

"That I almost had sex in the back seat of a truck like some hormone-driven teenager?"

"No." Feeling unreasonably good for a man who only minutes before had been perched on the rocky edge of a precipice, Gavin skimmed a finger down the slope of her nose. "Tell her you were casting a spell on me."

Tara couldn't help it. She smiled.

"I'll pick you up tomorrow night at seven. Oh, and dress casually. This is Whiskey River, not trendy San Francisco. Jeans will be fine."

Ten minutes later, as she gave the Realtor a tour of the inside of the house, Tara passed by a gilt-framed mirror and realized she was still smiling.

The midnight sky was a vast sea of black velvet scattered with diamonds. Ice crystals sparkled in the frosty night air as Brianna made her way through the forest, following a siren's call older than time. She was the other side of her twin sister Morganna, the quiet witch, the temperate, logical one.

Born to be unrelentingly generous and loving, she'd certainly never invite down the dark forces to slay her enemies. Nor would she respond to such primitive forces as fury, or lust. Her sole purpose in life was to create order out of a world that seemed to grow more chaotic with each passing day. It was not in her nature to behave rashly.

Yet, she was out in the wintery night, planning to meet the mortal man she'd not been able to get out of her mind.

He was waiting for her, standing all alone in the circle of sacred oak. He was clad all in black — dark to her light, male to her female.

Without saying a word, he pushed her white fur hood back and gathered a fistful of her red-

gold hair in his hand while his free hand deftly unfastened the diamond button of the cape and pushed it off her shoulders.

She stood before him, totally naked, save for the ancient silver-and-jet amulet around her throat. He pulled her toward him for a long minute and kissed her passionately, before lowering her onto her cape.

He knelt beside her. "You are so lovely." He drank deeply from her parted lips. Somewhere in the tops of the trees an owl hooted, a sad and lonely sound that made them even more glad to have each other. It began to snow, soft white flakes that drifted down like feathers shaken from some giant god's goose-down pillow, but steeped in the magic of the night, of each other, Brianna and her mortal lover didn't feel the cold as the flakes covered them like a pristine white quilt.

"Damn." Gavin swore as he threw down the pen, leaned back in his chair and closed his eyes. Brianna had always been the boring, passive sister. Until tonight, when somehow she'd taken on Tara's personality and had him envisioning hot, carnal scenes that his editors would never, in a million years, allow.

His body ached, and Gavin didn't need to look down to know that it was reacting to the erotic mind pictures. What the hell was happening to him? If he didn't know better, he thought with grim amusement, he'd think that Tara Delaney — or that crafty old Brigid — really *had* cast a spell on him.

He dragged a hand down his face, then studied the frames he'd drawn. If it *was* a spell, he supposed he shouldn't complain. After all, in the entire scheme of things, a perpetual hard-on wasn't such a bad price to pay for some of the best work of his career.

The following morning, after yet another restless night filled with creaking floors, scratching tree branches and erotic dreams, Tara was in the Whiskey River mercantile, pushing her cart through aisles filled with ripe orange pumpkins and displays of candy, costumes and candles set up for Halloween.

In ancient times, Celts had prepared feasts for the departed souls who'd be walking among them during this holy time of ending and beginning. Some of her happiest childhood memories revolved around this joyous time of parties and bonfires.

Tara took a bag of miniature chocolate bars from a display and put them into her cart. She doubted that any local youngsters would dare trick-or-treat at the witch's haunted house. But if they did, she intended to be prepared.

When she felt someone staring at her, she slowly turned around. There, standing beside a pyramid of pumpkins, was an elderly man whose rotund body, pink cheeks and snowy beard were reminiscent of Santa Claus. She thought he seemed vaguely familiar, then realized he'd been one of the customers at the diner the other morning.

"I'm sorry," he said when he realized he'd attracted her attention. "I didn't mean to stare." He closed the distance between them, allowing her to catch a whiff of cherry pipe tobacco. "It's just that when I saw you, I had this sudden feeling of déjà vu. It was as if fifty years of my life had just whirled away."

His blue eyes were twinkling at her in a way that encouraged Tara to smile back. "You knew my grandmother, Brigid Delaney," she guessed.

"I was in love with her for half a century."

"Really?" Tara gave him a longer, more critical glance. She wondered why, if he and her grandmother had been as close, Brigid had never mentioned him. "I'm sorry, I'm afraid I don't know your name."

"Forgive me for not introducing myself. I'm Reginald McVey. And you are, of course, the lovely Tara. Your grandmother spoke of you often. She was very proud of all your accomplishments."

"So I keep hearing." Realizing that her tone was sharper than it need be, she forced another smile and tried again. "Have you lived in Whiskey River all those years, Mr. McVey?"

"Off and on. I'm afraid I'm a bit of a travelin' man. Caught the wanderlust at an early age and couldn't shake it. I think that's one of the reasons Brigid refused to marry me. She was happy here in Whiskey River."

"She was that. Were you visiting her when she died?"

He frowned and his bright blue eyes shadowed. "Unfortunately, I've been in the Himalayas — Tibet, Nepal, India — for the past nine months. I only arrived in town last week to bring Brigid a present —

a Tibetan singing bowl. I was devastated to learn of her tragic accident."

"It was tragic," Tara agreed with a sigh. "And certainly unexpected." She shook off the sadness that always came when she thought of her grandmother falling down those stairs. Had she lain on the landing, broken and frightened? Or had she died instantly? She had forgotten to ask the sheriff, but it didn't really make any difference. Not now.

"I'm staying at the Silver Spur," Reginald McVey volunteered, pulling Tara out of her depressing thoughts. "I assume you've come to claim your inheritance?"

"You know about that?"

"Your grandmother may not have been willing to marry me, but she did confide in me. She told me five years ago that she was planning to leave the house and all its contents to you."

"With a caveat," Tara muttered.

"I don't understand."

"I'd planned to sell the house. Still do, as a matter of fact. But first I have to live in it for a month."

"One cycle of the moon." He threw back his snowy head and laughed, a deep booming belly laugh that made her think that he could probably make a fortune hiring himself out at Christmas parties. "If that isn't just like the crafty old witch, finding a way to force you to face your other inheritance."

Knowing he was referring to her genetic inheritance, Tara didn't answer. Although it was obvious that he was indeed a close friend of her grandmother's, she definitely wasn't in the mood to discuss her aversion to witchcraft.

"Well, I'd love to visit longer, but I'm afraid my ice cream's beginning to melt," she said.

"I'm sorry." The color in his ruddy cheeks deepened further. "I'm going to be leaving town soon — I have a cruise scheduled to the Greek Isles — but if you don't mind, I'd very much appreciate the opportunity to drop by the house and give you the bowl. I've carried it a very long way and would like to know that at least Brigid's granddaughter was enjoying it."

Terrific. That's all she needed. One more knickknack to deal with. Not wanting to disappoint him, Tara smiled. "I'd like that," she agreed.

After inviting him to drop by anytime, she continued shopping and was standing in the bread aisle, trying to decide between the wheat bagels and honey cinnamon ones, when a young woman approached.

"I hate to disturb you," she said hesitantly, "but are you Brigid Delaney's granddaughter?"

"I'm Tara Delaney." Tara felt every muscle in her body tense as she waited for the inevitable request. She did not have to wait long.

"I'm Vicki Harper. And I wanted to tell you how sorry I was about your grandmother passing away. It must have come as a terrible shock, as vital as Brigid seemed to be."

"Thank you. Yes, it was unexpected." Tara began to relax. Too soon, she discovered.

"Are you here in Whiskey River to pick up her practice?"

"No." Tara's tone was firm. Final.

"Oh, that's too bad. I realize now that we probably overworked the poor dear something awful, but we all cared for her so much. And she provided so much comfort. You should hear the changes she made in Iris Johnson's life."

"I heard."

"And there were so many others. Too many to count. I don't know what we're all going to do without her." She sighed and gave Tara a long, disappointed look that spoke volumes.

"I don't do magic," Tara said as the silence settled over them. "Or cast spells. But if you need someone to talk to about a personal problem —"

"Oh, would you?" Hope shone in the woman's eyes. And even as she felt herself being pulled into a situation she'd spent her entire life avoiding, Tara had a sixth sense that her grandmother was smiling her approval.

"I'd be so appreciative. Brigid was such a good listener."

"Yes, she was."

"You know, although I truly believed in her powers, there were times I thought that a lot of her success in turning lives around was due to her ability to listen. And helping people find their own solutions to their problems."

That was much the same thing Iris had said when she'd told Tara about the self-affirming words Brigid had instructed her to repeat each morning.

"I think you may be right." Tara recalled all too vividly how well her grandmother had listened to her after the Richard debacle. She looked into her grocery cart and pictured the Ben & Jerry's Cherry Garcia ice cream continuing to melt while Vicki Harper related her life story. "Why don't I finish up my shopping," she suggested, "and I'll meet you at my house in about an hour."

"That'd be wonderful. Thank you." Obviously overflowing with renewed hope, Vicki reached out and hugged Tara. Then hurried away, as if afraid her newfound benefactor would change her mind.

Tara watched her go, fearing that by agreeing to talk with Vicki Harper, she might be opening a door that she'd vowed to leave closed. But although she might have turned her back on magic, she didn't have it in her to turn away a person in trouble. Even if that person's needs conflicted with her own.

"If I didn't know any better, Grandy," she muttered as she tossed the honey cinnamon bagels into the cart, "I'd suspect this was just another example of your interference."

Tara realized she'd spoken out loud when a passing man gave her a sideways glance, then hurried on. Instead of being embarrassed, Tara merely laughed. Eccentric behavior was undoubtedly considered de rigueur for witches in Whiskey River.

9

Vicki Harper had obviously never heard the axiom that brevity was the soul of wit. Over countless cups of orange spiced tea, she related the tale of her teenage romance with the town's so-called bad boy, who'd eventually grown up, settled down and become, of all things, a minister.

Vicki had graduated from cosmetology school, married the Reverend Jimmy Harper and had taken a part-time job doing hair at the Shear Pleasures beauty salon.

She stressed that her husband was a loving, caring man. Their marriage was perfect. Their life was perfect.

"It sounds as if you're a very lucky woman," Tara said, refilling their cups for the umpteenth time.

"I am. Which is why I feel so guilty about complaining. I keep thinking that God will punish me for wanting more when I already have so much."

"I'm sure it doesn't work that way," Tara said gently.

"That's what Jimmy says." Vicki sighed and dumped another spoon of sugar into her already sweetened tea. "But how does anyone know, really?"

When Vicki's blue eyes misted with unshed tears, Tara put her hand over the woman's trembling one. "You want children." It was an educated guess.

"So much." Vicki hitched in a breath. "I had my first ovary removed because of cysts when I was a senior in high school. The doctor wants to take the other, but I can't let him. Not until I try Brigid's remedy. I know three friends who swear they were only able to have children after they received the magic herbs from her."

"Does your husband know you're asking me for help?"

"Of course." She took the tissue Tara handed her and began drying her wet face. "Jimmy and I have never kept secrets from each other."

"And he doesn't mind?" Although several of Whiskey River's citizens seemed not only tolerant but eager to have a witch living among them, Tara couldn't imagine a minister being pleased about his wife seeking magical means to conceive a child.

"He's Unitarian," Vicki said, as if that

explained everything. "They're very open-minded."

Apparently so. Even as Tara reminded herself that she did not want to get involved, she viewed the pain in the woman's glistening blue eyes and made her decision.

"Wait here," she said. "I'll see what I can find."

The joy on Vicki Harper's face could have lit up all of Whiskey River for a month.

Tara went into Brigid's greenhouse and found some dried dragonwort and acorns that she wrapped up in a cream linen square, and tied it with a green ribbon, which symbolized fertility. Then she went into the study, opened an antique hand-carved box that her grandmother had discovered at a crossroads fair in the west counties of Ireland, and took out a small jade stone and a green votive candle.

"Keep this beneath your pillow," she said, handing Vicki the small linen package. "And keep this stone with you at all times."

"Oh!" Vicki's eyes widened as Tara put it into her palm. "It's so warm."

"Yes, it is, isn't it?" The stone, like so many things in the house, radiated with

Brigid's life force. "I think it's going to be a very powerful aid." She handed Vicki the sweet marjoram-scented candle. "Burn this when you're planning to make love, and keep it burning afterward."

"Oh, thank you!" Vicki Harper's relief was so palpable, Tara could have reached out and touched it.

"I can't guarantee anything —"

"Oh, I know that. But you've no idea how wonderful it is to have my hope renewed. And I just know it's going to work." She rubbed the jade stone between her palms, soaking up the warmth before slipping it into the pocket of her denim skirt. "How much do I owe you?"

"Nothing."

"But —"

"Consider it a gift from a friend."

"We don't know each other."

"We didn't," Tara corrected. "But I'd say that your telling me how you lost your virginity when you were sixteen in the back of Jimmy's father's pickup classifies me as a friend."

"Jimmy would just die if he knew I told you about that." Vicki giggled, sounding for the first time since Tara had met her like a young girl. "I was picking hay out of my hair for days." Her expression turned earnest again. "But really, I'd like to give you something. After all, I'd planned to pay your grandmother."

"My grandmother was in the business of selling her herbs. I'm not."

Vicki nodded sadly. "That's too bad," she said finally. "Because I think you're a natural."

With that she was gone, taking her herbs and candles with her.

Sighing, Tara wondered how long it would take for the erroneous word to get out that Brigid Delaney's granddaughter had finally showed up to take over her grandmother's house. And the family business.

For a woman known for making cool, calculated decisions, Tara dithered uncharacteristically over what to wear on what she could no longer deny was a date. Gavin had told her that jeans were appropriate, but a strong feminine vanity she'd thought she'd packed away with her wedding gown and veil returned with a vengeance, making her want to look her best.

No, she decided as she discarded one possible choice after another, she wanted to look even *better* than her best. It would be a simple matter to cast a spell over him, but using magic to achieve her wishes had never been Tara's way. If she was going to charm Gavin, she was going to do it on her own merits.

Not that she really wanted to charm him.

Oh, hell, she admitted, of course she did.

Reminding herself that her response to the man was only female hormones running amuck — after all, she hadn't allowed herself to even feel attracted to any man since the Richard debacle — she went upstairs to the attic.

Like the rest of the house, the attic was overflowing with Brigid's personal belongings. Tara knew that several of the steamer trunks — and the clothes inside them — had come all the way from Ireland long before Tara's mother was born.

When she'd been a little girl, Tara had enjoyed playing dress-up in the hats and turn-of-the century dresses that had belonged to her great-grandmother, Moira. The first Delaney woman to step foot in America, Moira had left her beloved county Clare one step ahead of the rigid priest who'd threatened to excommunicate her for practicing witchcraft.

The clothes were all carefully wrapped in tissue and carried the faint scent of mothballs. They were also dangerously fragile, making Tara fear they'd crumble to dust if she tried to wear them.

She was getting discouraged when one particular item captured her eye. High-collared and long-sleeved, the blouse was created of a lace so delicate it could have been spun by fairies from dandelion fluff. Instead of the camphor scent that had been prevalent in the other trunks, the blouse carried a faint scent of the sachet that had been tucked into the tissue it had been lovingly wrapped in.

Tara lifted the blouse to her nose, breathed in the fresh, green, rain-washed fragrance of the Irish countryside and imagined her great-grandmother wearing this blouse to dinner in a pub with one of her admirers after a performance. Moira Delaney had been her country's premiere actress, renowned for her beauty, talent, sharp wit and even sharper tongue, which tended to get her in trouble when she spoke up for women's rights. In a country where female equality had not been a burning issue, she'd been infamous for her independent mind and free-spirited life-style.

Like the jade stone Tara had given Vicki earlier, the blouse practically hummed with the energy of the woman who'd once worn it. Deciding she could use all the emotional and psychic help she could get to protect her from Gavin's own form of masculine magic, Tara took it downstairs with her.

Gavin had known Tara was lovely. But he was not prepared for the vision who opened the door of Brigid's house. She'd complied with his suggestion to wear jeans. But the feelings stirred by what she'd chosen to wear with those snug blue jeans were a long, long way from being casual.

"You look absolutely gorgeous."

Unreasonably nervous, but loath to show it, Tara laced her fingers together behind her back. Gavin wondered if she knew how the gesture only served to pull the snug lace tighter against the soft globes of her breasts.

"The blouse belonged to my great-grandmother." She absently ran her hand down the front of the lace bodice. "She was an actress in Ireland. When I was getting dressed earlier, I couldn't help wondering if she'd worn this on the stage."

Hands in his pockets, Gavin rocked back on his heels and looked at her. She'd done something to her face, too. There was a touch of soft rose in her cheeks and some smoky color around her eyes that gave them a sultry, siren's look. Although she'd applied it with a light touch, this was the first time he'd seen her wearing makeup. Gavin found the fact that she'd made an extra effort with her appearance encouraging.

"If she had been wearing that, she would have had the audience eating out of the palm of her hand."

Although their relationship — and she was beginning to have to admit that they had one, of sorts — had been rocky from the start, Tara smiled. It was one of the first honest ones she'd given him. "That's exactly what I was thinking.

"If you want to come in for a minute, I'll get my coat," she suggested when he just kept standing there, studying her as a botanist might study some exotic new breed of orchid.

He followed her into the parlor, which was a great deal neater than it had been the last time he'd been here. "You've been working hard."

She glanced around the room, which, since having been cleaned, was cheery and neat. "I didn't have much choice. Call me picky, but I draw the line at sharing my living space with spiders."

"Makes sense to me." He picked up a cut-glass globe. "Ah, a crystal ball." He stared down into it. "I don't suppose you'd be willing to look into it and tell my future?"

Once again Tara proved she had the capacity to surprise him. "Of course."

When she held out her hand for the globe, he laughed. "I was just kidding around."

"Ah, but I wasn't."

They stood a few feet apart, Gavin holding one of Brigid's collection of gazing balls, Tara with her hand outstretched. Neither moved until finally, deciding that it might prove entertaining if nothing else, Gavin placed the crystal sphere on her palm.

"I see a man," she murmured dramatically, tracing her fingertips over the crystal surface. "A creative man who is often misunderstood."

"So far, so good."

"A man who enjoys the better things in life."

"Guilty."

"A man accustomed to fast cars, good wine and beautiful, willing women in his life. And his bed."

"Bingo," he said, playing along. She'd hit

the old Gavin Thomas right on the money. He decided that there was no point in revealing that the only women in his life these days, besides Tara, were Brianna and Morganna. As for females warming his bed, as Trace had so succinctly pointed out over breakfast right before Tara had shown up in Whiskey River, it had been a very long time since he'd gotten lucky.

Not that he hadn't had more than his share of feminine offers. But having learned the hard way that sex could end up getting a guy in deep trouble, he hadn't met any woman worth the risk. Until Tara.

"And I see a woman."

"Tell me she's a drop-dead gorgeous redhead with remarkable green eyes, and I'll be in your debt for life."

"She has red hair," Tara agreed. There was no way she was going to let him know that having him refer to her as drop-dead gorgeous was enough to start her blood humming. "And her eyes are green."

"Like the sea. Calm and inviting one minute, stormy and dangerous the next. The type of eyes a guy could drown in. And relish the experience."

His voice had dropped to the lower registers. Tara lowered her gaze to the ball and was startled by the image that was emerging from the previously clear globe.

An image of Gavin and her together. Her head was tilted back, enticing his lips to taste her throat. Her eyes were closed, and her hands were gathering up fistfuls of his shirt while his own fingers were busy on the pearl buttons of her blouse.

"The woman has been waiting for the man for a very long time," she murmured.

"He's sorry to have kept her waiting."

"He should be." Tara put the globe down onto the marble-topped side table and picked up her jacket from the back of a chair. "Because she's starving."

As she moved toward the door, Gavin made the mistake of glancing down at the crystal globe. The vision surrounded by swirling clouds of fog was every bit as sexy as it was unexpected. And even as he felt his body growing hard at the idea of being with Tara in such an erotic fashion, Gavin assured himself that the picture he knew would remain forever stamped in his memory was merely a trick of lighting. That and a result of his rampant imagination and runaway testosterone.

When Gavin pulled into the parking lot of the large, two-story building, Tara suffered a moment's trepidation. The name

Denim and Diamonds flashed in bright lights above the door.

Accustomed to trendy San Francisco night spots, where the jazz was cool and the wine list boasted the best Napa Valley had to offer, Tara couldn't remember the last time she'd been in a cowboy bar. Actually, she realized as Gavin went around the front of the truck to open the passenger door, she'd *never* been in a cowboy bar.

Gavin sensed her hesitation. "There's plenty of time to drive to Payson or Flag-staff."

If it was a test, Tara was determined to pass it. Besides, it occurred to her that this was undoubtedly the same place Brigid had danced the Texas Two-Step with Thatcher Reardon.

Still intrigued by that idea, Tara threw caution to the wind. "I can't think of any place I'd rather be."

As she walked with him toward the heavy oak door into which brands of local ranches had been burned, Tara imagined she could hear her grandmother's pleased, satisfied laughter.

Except for the extensive collection of sports memorabilia displayed in a glass case just inside the door, the inside of Denim and Diamonds was decidedly Western.

"The place recently changed hands," Gavin explained. "A former pro athlete from Phoenix bought it when he and his wife moved to Whiskey River about six months ago. He added a sports bar with satellite television in the back, turned the upstairs into dining rooms, but kept the downstairs as a watering hole for the locals."

"Sounds as if the new owner's got all the bases covered," she murmured, glancing past him into the bar, where a young man wearing a cowboy hat and a young woman with a tight leather skirt and rhinestone-studded Western-cut blouse were deftly making their way through a series of remarkably complex dance steps.

"Wrong sport."

She tried to imagine her grandmother dancing that way with Thatcher Reardon and failed. "Excuse me?"

"Covering the bases is baseball. Nick McGraw's game was football. He was a quarterback for the Phoenix Thunderbirds."

"Oh." She shrugged, having scant interest in professional sports or the men who played them. "Well, he obviously made a wise investment."

"Thanks," a deep voice behind her said. Tara turned around and found herself gazing into the handsome face of a man who appeared to be in his mid-forties. "I keep assuring myself that buying the place was more than merely a typical mid-life crisis." He held out his hand. "I'm Nick McGraw."

Tara found herself immediately liking this man with the friendly eyes set in a dark, sun-weathered face. "Tara Delaney."

"Ah, Brigid's granddaughter." His gaze swept over her. "I suppose you're accustomed to people telling you that you bear a striking family resemblance to her."

"Not really." She didn't mention that with the exception of Richard, whom she'd been going to marry, she'd never introduced any of her San Francisco friends to her grandmother.

"You do," Nick confirmed. "She was a remarkable woman."

"Yes, she was." Tara wondered if Nick was one of his grandmother's customers. She did not have to wonder long.

"She gave me some salve for my knees that really helped my arthritis. Even my wife, who's a doctor, was impressed."

Tara was not at all surprised by that little medical bulletin. "My grandmother seemed to have a very thriving practice here in Whiskey River."

"She sure kept busy," Nick agreed. His gaze became speculative. "I don't suppose you're —"

"No." Tara cut him off with a shake of her head. "I have no plans to take over the business."

"Too bad." He shrugged his wide shoulders. "Whiskey River is one of those small towns where everyone has a role to play. Brigid's death has left a pretty big void in the community."

"I'm sorry, Mr. McGraw, but I already have a life back in San Francisco."

"So I've heard. Brigid was very proud of you. I doubt there's anyone in town who hasn't had your letters read to them."

Letters that had become less and less frequent these past two years, Tara thought miserably.

Watching the shadow move across her eyes, Gavin decided the time had come to change the subject. "Is our table ready, Nick?"

"Sure." The former football star flashed Tara an apologetic smile. "Sorry to hold you up. I really just wanted to tell you that I'm sorry for your loss. And I miss Brigid's friendship. If it's any consolation, Ms.

Delaney, your grandmother was much loved here in Whiskey River."

"So I've discovered, Mr. McGraw. It's a comfort to know she had so many friends."

"She sure did." His smile reached his eyes, crinkling the corners in an attractive way. "And it's Nick."

"And I'm Tara." Going by Ms. Delaney seemed ridiculous in Whiskey River, and especially ridiculous here in the casual atmosphere of Denim and Diamonds.

Without any further delay, Nick led them up the stairs. "It was my wife Laurel's idea to tear out the walls up here and turn the bedrooms into dining rooms," he said as they walked down the hallway. "I have to admit I had my doubts, but so far most of the tables are booked nearly every night."

"Was this originally a hotel?"

"Not exactly." Nick exchanged a grin with Gavin. "Most of the rooms were rented by the hour."

"Oh."

Although she'd always thought of herself as a sophisticated woman, Tara could feel the color warming her cheeks as she entered a room that was definitely decorated in early bordello. The wallpaper was red flocked velvet; paintings of fleshy nudes had been hung on the scarlet-as-sin walls. The paintings didn't disturb her. But the lingering erotic vibrations were decidedly unsettling.

Gavin immediately noticed her discomfort. "If you want to go somewhere else —"

"Of course not. I've never eaten in a bordello before. Brigid used to say that you should strive to learn one thing, or have one new experience, every day."

"That sure sounds like her," Nick agreed. "I don't think I've ever met a more adventurous lady."

He plucked two tasseled menus from a rack by the door and led them to a table situated in front of a wide stone fireplace. Tara was faintly amused when a bit of masculine jockeying occurred over who'd hold the heavy oak chair out for her. In the end, his eyes laughing as if he was enjoying himself immensely, Nick backed away and surrendered the role of gallant to Gavin.

"Heather will be your waitress tonight. If there's anything I can take care of personally, be sure and let me know." He flashed her a smile that made her think that there'd undoubtedly been a time when he'd probably scored quite well off the gridiron as well as on. "Tara, it was a pleasure meeting you. I hope I'll see you again before you leave town."

"I think you can count on that," Tara assured him. "If the food tastes even half as good as it looks, I have a feeling I'm going to be a regular." Passing the other tables, she'd been impressed by the appearance and aromas of the other diners' meals.

"We aim to please," Nick assured her. "And later, if you feel like some exercise to work off your meal, Randy and Mallory will be giving some country dance lessons downstairs."

Tara guessed Randy and Mallory were the couple who'd been whirling around the dance floor in the bar. "I'll keep it in mind," she murmured, having no such plans.

"Liar," Gavin said when they were alone again.

"I have no idea what you're talking about."

He laughed, enjoying the challenge her guarded tone presented. "You have no intention of dancing with me." Despite her renewed coolness, he reached out and took hold of her hand. "I'm making you nervous again."

"That's not it at all." She refused to give him the satisfaction of tugging her hand away. Better to pretend that his touch meant nothing to her. "I just don't relish the idea of making a fool of myself."

"It's not that difficult. If you'd surrender your need to control everything for just a little while and let me lead, it'd be a snap."

Since it was true, she decided not to challenge his remark about her need for control. "I should have suspected from your accent that you'd be familiar with country music," she said instead.

"It's like mother's milk to us down-home Texas boys. It's also about as much fun as you can have standing up," he coaxed.

After the kisses they'd shared, Tara thought there was definitely room for argument on that point. "I'm not used to following."

"Now why doesn't that surprise me?" His lips curved and the light in his eyes was surprisingly friendly. Tara felt herself relaxing for the first time with this man.

"I'll think about it." Heaven help her, as the enticing music filtered up the stairs, she found herself actually considering the idea. After all, if Brigid could do it . . .

"You do that." He lifted their linked hands to his lips and brushed a kiss against her knuckles. "The night's still young."

His gaze, rife with masculine intentions,

met her guarded one, and held. The way his pupils darkened in the flickering light from the candle between them, Tara realized that once again they were sharing the same thoughts. Thoughts too intimate, too sensual, for such a public place.

Her mind clouded, her blood heated, her heart raced. She couldn't remember ever being so affected by the mere presence of a man. Even Richard, who'd broken her heart, hadn't had the power to make her feel as if she were drowning.

In a blinding moment of realization Tara knew that she'd been wrong. Richard couldn't have broken her heart because, in truth, she hadn't given it to him. All he'd done was publicly humiliate her, which at the time had seemed horribly painful.

But this man . . . She stared at his mouth, which she imagined she could still taste, and realized that no matter how much she might deny it, her life had unalterably changed the day she'd decided to come to Whiskey River to claim her inheritance.

10

So intent was she on trying to sort out her whirling thoughts, Tara failed to notice the arrival of a pretty brunette at their table.

"Hi," she said with a friendly smile that reminded Tara vaguely of a cheerleader. "Can I get you guys something to drink?"

Her mind still wrapped in a warm sensual fog, Tara merely stared up at her.

"Tara?" Gavin felt more than a little satisfied. He'd wanted a reaction and he'd gotten it. Of course, he hadn't counted on the rush of tenderness he felt as confusion flooded into her eyes and vulnerability softened her exquisitely lovely features.

She blinked. A slow, distracted blink that pulled at a thousand unnamed cords inside him.

"Would you like a drink?"

His tone was warm and gentle, calming and exciting her at the same time. It was the voice of her dreams. She could have listened to it forever.

"I think . . ." What was wrong with her? She made decisions worth millions of dollars every day. And now, all it took was a hot look from a sexy man who couldn't be more wrong for her to wipe her mind as clear as glass.

She gave herself a stiff mental shake. "I'd like a glass of merlot, please," she said.

"Merlot for the lady," Heather said, writing the order down. "Gavin? The usual?"

Gavin decided that something a little more special than draft beer was required on a night that seemed destined to alter a guy's life. "I'll have what the lady's having. In fact, why don't you bring us a bottle?"

"Sure. You want a wine list?"

"Nah. Just tell Nick I want the best he's got."

"You got it." With the promise of a hefty tip dancing in her cornflower blue eyes, Heather practically skipped away from the table.

"Have I told you that you look gorgeous tonight?" Gavin asked when they were alone again.

"I believe you mentioned it." The admiration in his dark gaze made her feel unreasonably nervous. Needing something to do, she spent an inordinately long time spreading the white napkin over her lap.

"If your great-grandmother looked anything like you do sitting here in the candle-light, I can definitely imagine why all the men in Ireland were supposedly in love with her."

She glanced up at him with surprise. "All right, that cinches it. Obviously you and Brigid really were friends." She knew her grandmother, while outwardly gregarious, had still held family secrets close.

"She was at a point in her life when people tend to look back. I guess she found me a good listener."

Once again Tara felt a pang of guilt that she hadn't been there to listen to her grandmother's stories. Never mind that she'd heard them all a thousand times.

"What did she tell you about Moira?"

"That she was the most popular actress of her day, as beloved in her country as Lily Langtree was in Great Britain. That, although she never married, she enjoyed the company of men as both friends and lovers. And that her free-spirited behavior was the theme of more than a few Sunday sermons."

"I've always admired Moira's courage," Tara said. "She was thirty when she got pregnant with my grandmother, which was, back then, an age when females were considered spinsters."

"It must not have been easy for her. A single woman alone in a time and country dominated by men."

"I think, from stories Brigid told me about her, that she actually enjoyed playing the role of rebel." Tara absently toyed with the lace cuff and wished, as she so often did, that she possessed just a tad of Moira's flair for living life to the fullest.

"There was, of course, an uproar from pulpits from Galway to Dublin. Children born out of wedlock were not unheard-of, even in nineteenth-century Ireland. But other women — proper women — didn't flaunt their behavior. And, of course, it didn't help that Moira refused to display regret for her sin."

"Gotta admire a woman of conviction."

Before Tara could answer, Heather returned with the wine. Gavin pronounced it fine; Heather filled their glasses and, after taking their orders, disappeared again.

"Brigid told me she came to this country when she was an infant," he said, picking up the conversation where they'd left off.

"That's right." Tara took a sip of the ruby wine and felt herself beginning to relax again. "After Moira, in her own inimitably rebellious style, refused to name her child's father."

"I'm surprised he didn't come forward to support her." He would have, Gavin thought. Whatever the cost. Of course, it was just such behavior that had landed him in hot water.

"He may have wanted to, but I can easily envision Moira refusing the offer," Tara allowed. "According to Grandy, her mother was unrelentingly independent. After all, if threats of excommunication couldn't get her to the altar, I'm not sure what difference a proposal would have made. If there was one. But I don't think there was, because my grandmother never mentioned it."

"Yet surely shotgun marriages weren't that uncommon?"

"Probably not. But we Delaney women seem to have a knack for falling for guys who aren't real big on commitment." Tara sighed as her mind flitted back to Richard. "Perhaps Moira decided being a happy single mother was preferable to being miserable spending her days with a former lover who felt trapped into matrimony."

"Not all men consider marriage a trap," Gavin felt obliged to point out as he thought of Trace and Mariah. He also conveniently neglected to add that only days ago he'd referred to it as a less-than-desirable institution.

"True." Tara smiled as she thought about her own parents. "My mother and father have a wonderful marriage. But I think they're the exception, rather than the rule.

"Anyway," she said, getting back to the subject of her colorful great-grandmother, "according to family lore, when rumors started about who the child's father might be, and the names of innocent men who were merely friends began being bandied around, Moira decided the time had come to seek her fortune in America."

"On the Great White Way."

"She had an incredibly successful career on Broadway. In fact, she was still head-lining in her seventies. Brigid followed in her theatrical footsteps, becoming a singer. But she never enjoyed the spotlight."

"Which was why, when a handsome cowboy performing in a rodeo at Madison Square Garden invited her to travel to Arizona with him, Brigid headed west," Gavin said, proving once again that Brigid had felt close enough to him to share her personal history.

"That's right. Unfortunately, although she hadn't inherited her mother's love of performing, she ended up choosing the same type of man. After the rodeo here in

Whiskey River, the cowboy moved on to Canada to ride bucking broncs at the Calgary Stampede."

"She could have gone with him," Gavin ventured.

"I suppose. Or, more likely, he never asked." Tara shrugged. "She always claimed she was destined to live here. Apparently, she felt instantly at home the first moment she stepped off the Santa Fe passenger train at the depot. So she stayed in Whiskey River and raised my mother, supporting them both with the proceeds of her writing and her herb business."

"Brigid told me that your mother broke with tradition by marrying. But your name is still Delaney."

"My mother kept her family name and passed it down to me." Tara smiled. "Some traditions are too strong to mess with."

He smiled back and she couldn't help noticing that it held considerable charm.

He took another drink of wine, eyeing her over the rim of the glass. "Do you have any idea," he asked, his voice dropping to its lowest registers, "how much I want to drag you beneath the table and risk getting us both kicked out of here?"

She opened her mouth to insist that it wouldn't be all that easy, then decided there was no point in trying to lie. Because, heaven help her, although the conversation about the Delaney women had proven a welcome distraction, she couldn't help wondering when he was going to kiss her again.

"It's Brigid," she insisted. "She's been pulling the strings from the beginning."

"I agree she might have been doing a little matchmaking by setting us up to meet in the first place. And insisting you stay in the house a month is a little suspicious. But believe me, sweetheart, your grandmother has nothing to do with the way I feel about you."

"That's what you think," she muttered. Strangely, talking about their shared desire succeeded in shattering the sensual mood, for now. More than a little relieved, Tara sat back and turned the conversation to Gavin's books.

Two hours later, after steaks so tender they practically melted in the mouth, baked potatoes piled high with sour cream and garnished with chives and peas that tasted as if they'd been grown in a local garden, they were lingering over coffee and the best white cheesecake she'd ever tasted.

As Gavin sipped his coffee and looked at

her across the table, he wondered if she had any idea how striking she was. She might not be larger than life, like her famed great-grandmother Moira, or outgoing and free-spirited like Brigid, but she definitely had inherited the Delaney women's ability to charm.

He'd been drawn, against his will, to Pamela. He'd also been, for a brief, soul-wrenching time, obsessed with that singularly amoral woman. But he'd always felt edgy around her. And although he wanted Tara no less than he had that first moment he'd seen her — and she still continued to represent one helluva risk — he found himself beginning to relax around her. To enjoy just being with her, watching her, listening to her.

Although he'd heard the story of her runaway fiancé, he still couldn't believe that all the available men — and probably a lot of the unavailable ones — in San Francisco weren't constantly coming to blows, trying to win this woman.

Obviously, he decided, spending your days in the business jungle weakened a guy's natural instinct for claiming a mate. Fortunately, Gavin's instincts were working just fine.

He was thinking about taking her home

and sharing some hot, sweaty sex when a couple stopped beside their table.

"Noel." He stood and embraced the woman clad in corduroy jeans and a flowing tunic woven in a traditional Navajo pattern. No small feat, since the advanced state of her pregnancy created a formidable physical barrier. "I swear, you get more gorgeous every day."

Watching Gavin bestow such easy affection on another woman caused something that felt uncomfortably like jealousy to stir deep inside Tara.

"You are such a silver-tongued devil, Gavin Thomas." The woman's delighted laughter reminded Tara of silver bells.

"It's the truth," Gavin said. The smile was still on his face as he turned to Tara. "Tara, may I introduce the sexiest pregnant woman in Whiskey River. Noel Giraudeau. Noel, this is —"

"Tara Delaney." Noel held out her hand. "I've only lived in Whiskey River a few months, but your grandmother and I had grown very close."

As she shook hands, Tara felt the unmistakable force flowing outward from Noel's fingertips and knew that there was a great deal more to this woman than met the eye. She exchanged a quick, startled look with Noel, whose own calm gaze silently assured her that she was not mistaken.

"Brigid had a lot of friends." Tara repeated what she'd been saying for days.

"Yes. She was a remarkable woman. And she loved you very, very much." Noel toyed absently with a dangling silver-and-turquoise earring as she slid a speculative gaze Gavin's way. Apparently receiving an answer to her unspoken question, she then turned toward the tall chestnut-haired man standing beside her.

"This is Mackenzie Reardon." The glow in her eyes and in her cheeks as she looked up at him had Tara regretting her earlier tinge of jealousy. Obviously, Noel Giraudeau had no designs on Gavin.

"Reardon?" He was a very attractive man, Tara decided, with his intelligent green eyes, square chin and broad shoulders. But his smile didn't affect her the way Gavin's did. And the touch of his hand as his fingers briefly enclosed hers, failed to heat her blood. "Are you any relation to Thatcher Reardon?"

"He's my father."

Tara thought she detected a faint resemblance, but it was more in the easy self-confidence both men shared than outward appearances. "Are you an attorney, too?"

"No, I'm in the newspaper business. I own the *Rim Rock Record*."

"Mac used to be city editor of the *Chicago Sun-Times*," Noel revealed with obvious feminine pride. "But he decided to give up the rat race and return home to his roots."

He laughed and slipped his arm around what remained of Noel's waist. "And you've no idea how glad I am that I did."

They exchanged laughing looks filled with such love that Tara felt as if she were intruding on a private moment.

"Giraudeau," she murmured as the name sunk in. "Aren't you —"

"The pregnant princess," Noel filled in the tabloid headline cheerfully. "That's me. In the flesh." She laughed as she ran her palms over her bulging stomach. Tara couldn't help noticing that she was not wearing a wedding ring. "And so much flesh, too."

"And every inch of it beautiful," Mac assured her.

Although Tara was not a follower of celebrity gossip, a person would have had to have spent the past few months on another galaxy not to have heard the story of Princess Noel Giraudeau of Montacroix's broken engagement to her childhood sweetheart.

Noel had always been described as the ice princess, in comparison to her sultry older sister, Chantal, and her uncharacteristic behavior had garnered more than a little attention from the paparazzi. When she'd turned up in America, pregnant and unmarried, the news sent shock waves rippling throughout the world.

"Your coffee's getting cold," Noel said. She placed a hand on Tara's arm. "I'd love to have a chance to chat. Why don't you come to tea Friday afternoon? About three?"

"I'd love to have tea with you, Princess."

"Oh, please." Noel rolled her expressive blue eyes. "Royalty is definitely out of place in Whiskey River. Please call me Noel." She took a small embossed card from her purse. "Here's the address of my gallery. You can't miss it. It's on Main Street, between the newspaper office and the mercantile."

"The Road to Ruin." Tara had seen it when she'd come out of the mercantile.

"It's a long story," Noel said with another of her light silvery laughs when Tara mentioned having been intrigued by the gallery's name. "I'll tell you all about it Friday."

She went up on her toes and brushed a light kiss against Gavin's cheek. "Good luck," she whispered for his ears only. Then she left the dining room, hand in hand with Mackenzie Reardon.

"Well, I certainly never would have expected to meet a European princess in Whiskey River," Tara said.

"As Noel said, royalty doesn't carry much weight here."

"She seems nice."

"She's the best." Gavin smiled, recalling her encouraging words.

Tara wondered if he knew the princess was blessed with the gift of second sight. "Are she and Mackenzie Reardon going to get married?"

"If he has anything to say about it. Noel keeps insisting she wants to wait until after the baby's born. It'd be my guess that she's worried he might not understand all he's taking on, but all you have to do is look at the guy to tell he's head over heels in love with her."

"And she with him," Tara murmured. "So he's not the baby's father?"

"No. Apparently he died."

"It couldn't have been all that long ago. I can see why she'd want to wait before rushing into things."

Gavin shrugged. "Since we've managed to get through an entire evening without a single argument, I hate to disagree with you, but I have to take Mac's side on this one. When people belong together, I don't see much point in waiting."

He had, Tara admitted privately, a point. And in truth, she'd never seen a couple who so obviously belonged together.

Unless, an errant little voice in the back of her mind suggested, *it's you and Gavin.*

Shut up, Grandy, Tara retorted.

It was obvious that Noel Giraudeau and Mackenzie Reardon shared a deep and abiding love. While what she and Gavin were experiencing was lust, pure and simple.

And Tara had no intention of allowing her grandmother to try to convince her otherwise.

Despite her earlier protestations, Tara proved that she was a good sport by going downstairs after dinner and dancing to the country-and-western band Nick had discovered playing in a Flagstaff bar. Gavin was right, she admitted as he twirled her through the steps — so long as she let him lead, she managed to keep from making a fool of herself.

It was when the music slowed that she

got into real trouble. Smiling with satisfaction at the change of pace, Gavin drew her to him, fitting her slender curves against the rigid male lines of his body. As she linked her fingers together behind his neck, it crossed Tara's mind that they were, at least in this way, a perfect fit.

Gavin rested his chin against her hair, inhaling a spicy scent that reminded him slightly of the potpourri Brigid had given him as a welcoming gift when he'd first arrived in Whiskey River.

When he pressed his lips against her silken hair, she sighed. When he spread his fingers against her back, warming her flesh beneath the antique lace, she tensed momentarily, then softened. Body, mind and heart.

"This is nice," he murmured against her ear. Actually, nice didn't begin to cover it. It was, he decided as he nuzzled her fragrant neck, pretty damn near perfect.

"Nice," she agreed, drawing in a quick, shaky breath when his teeth tugged gently on her earlobe.

The singer up on the nearby stage was singing the tale of a love between a man and woman that was predestined to last a lifetime. As she drifted contentedly in Gavin's arms, Tara found herself wishing desperately that she could believe in such a thing.

There had been a time, when she was younger, that Tara had believed every couple were like her mother and father. That people married not just because they were in love — whatever that meant — but because they were devoted to each other.

Her friends' divorces, plus her own experience with Richard, had led Tara to the unhappy conclusion that her parents were an anomaly. It was then she'd decided to adopt one aspect shared by all the other Delaney women save her mother.

She'd spend her life alone. But never lonely. Her life would be full. It would have meaning. She just wouldn't have a husband. Or children.

Although that was her plan, carefully conceived, logical to a fault, she hadn't been prepared for the low ache created deep in her most feminine core at the sight of the very pregnant Noel. Although it was a cliché, the woman had literally glowed.

Gavin tilted his head back and looked down into her face. "Something wrong?" he asked, noticing the faint lines marring her forehead.

"No." Looking up at him, reading the depth of emotion in his dark eyes, she allowed herself to relax and enjoy the wonder of his closeness, to go with the flow. "Everything's wonderful." She smiled as the romantic ballad seemed to swell inside her heart. "Actually, I can't remember when I've had a more perfect night."

"Not quite perfect," he murmured, gazing down at the lush lips he'd been waiting all evening to taste. "But I think we can get a little closer."

She did not have to possess second sight to realize Gavin's intention. Her eyes invited, her lips parted instinctively, as she watched his head slowly and deliberately lower.

Although he'd reminded himself that this was a public place, and despite the fact that he'd intended merely to give her a light kiss that would offer a promise of more to come, the moment his mouth touched hers, there was a flare of heat.

They both felt it jolting through them like electricity. As startled as she, he momentarily lifted his head, stared down at her and viewed the answering desire — and fear — in her remarkable eyes.

"Again," he murmured huskily.

"Again," she agreed in a low, throaty tone, even as she splayed her fingers against the back of his head and pulled his lips back to hers.

This time they were prepared for the shock. Lights still flashed behind the closed lids of her eyes, but Tara welcomed the dazzling kaleidoscope colors. Heat poured into his groin, but Gavin managed, just barely, to keep from dragging her into the nearest dark corner and ripping off her clothes. Their lips clung and held as they stood in the center of the dance floor, surrounded by the other couples moving around them.

Gradually, Gavin became aware of a hum of conversation. The crowd parted on either side of Tara and him as the dancers returned to their tables and waitresses hurried to take drink orders during the band's break.

"The music's stopped."

"Perhaps for you." She smiled dazedly up at him, reminding him vaguely of a woman sleepwalking. "But I still hear it."

He laughed, a bold, rich, satisfied sound, anticipating the music they'd spend the rest of the night making.

"Ready to leave?"

"Absolutely."

"Your place or mine?"

"Mine." Her smile turned her eyes to polished emeralds. "It's closer."

11

Tara's head cleared the moment they walked out of Denim and Diamonds into the October night. The mountain air was crisp and cold; a slight breeze blew away the cobwebs clouding her mind.

She could no longer deny what was happening between them. He wanted her, and she wanted him. They were two unattached individuals who wanted to jump each other's bones. If she'd been any other woman — any totally mortal woman — such shared desire should be simple.

Unfortunately, love had never been the slightest bit simple for the Delaney women.

Not that this was love, she reminded herself firmly.

Gavin pulled up in front of the house, cut the engine and pocketed the key. She'd been getting more tense with each mile until even his own nerves were beginning to feel the strain.

"I think I need to say something," she said softly.

"You've changed your mind." He could change it back again, Gavin knew. With just a touch of a fingertip here, a brush of his lips there. A few slow, deep kisses . . .

"No. Yes. Oh, hell." She dragged her hand through her hair. "You have to understand, I'm not like Brigid. Or Moira."

"So you keep telling me." He took hold of her hand after it made another sweep through her hair.

"I have a master's degree in business. I'm an M.B.A. And a C.P.A."

He managed, just barely, to keep from smiling at that. "So Brigid told me. She also said you're damn good at your work."

"I am." His thumb was stroking tantalizing circles on the sensitive skin of her palm, threatening to make her forget her carefully planned speech. "The point is, I've always felt the need for order in my life. For predictability."

"That can get a little boring." He lifted their joined hands and nibbled lightly at the fleshy part of her thumb.

"Not for me."

When his only response was a raised brow, she sighed. "All right, perhaps you're right. But I *like* boring. I like to map out my life. And I always stick to the plan."

"And I wasn't part of your life plan."

She made a sound that was part laugh, part groan. "Not hardly."

"How about this? Did you plan for this?"

He leaned over and captured her mouth with his with a force that would have caused her knees to buckle if she hadn't already been sitting down.

He dived into the kiss, into her, dragging her along with him, out where the emotional currents ran fast and deep. Logic deserted her as his dark taste sent her senses swimming. Reason, protests, were washed away by the ever-rising tide of desire. Breathless, she clung to him as she felt herself being pulled into the maelstrom.

Arousal pounded through him, hot and familiar. He wanted her beyond reason. Beyond sanity. He hadn't experienced such a visceral sense of need since Pamela, but this was somehow different. Because, he realized as he reluctantly surrendered her lips, Tara was different.

"Tell me that isn't worth a detour on your carefully mapped-out life." With a tenderness that was at direct odds with the powerful heat of his kiss, he trailed a finger around her lips. "You're right. This probably isn't the smartest thing either one of us has ever done. But I want you, Tara. And there's no way in hell you're going to convince me that you don't want me back. So are you really going to make both of us suffer another night of hot dreams?"

She knew what she should do. Tara took a deep breath, closed her eyes and tried to gather up what remained of her scattered wits. She looked up at him and slowly shook her head.

Gavin hadn't realized he'd been holding his breath until he felt the air escape his lungs on a long, relieved whoosh.

His arm was around her waist as they walked up onto the porch. Tara was grateful that people didn't lock their doors in Whiskey River; she wasn't certain she could have managed to get her key into the lock.

She turned on the light as she entered the front parlor. It took a minute for what Tara was seeing to sink in.

Gavin's curse was harsh and succinct. He glared at the room, which, only hours earlier, had been so tidy and now looked as if a hurricane had blown through it. The cushion on the red velvet chaise had been slashed, as had the upholstery on the matching wing chair. Drawers had been pulled out of the marble-topped end table, paintings had been ripped from their frames.

"Get back into the truck." Grabbing

hold of her arm, he dragged her from the house. "I'll call the sheriff."

One thing she'd always prided herself on sharing with the other Delaney women was her fierce spirit of independence. But as Tara watched Gavin calling on his cellular phone from the truck, his voice low and angry but controlled, she had to admit that she was more than a little grateful for his presence.

"It shouldn't be long," he said after he'd hung up. "Wait here, I'm going to go back in and make sure the bastards aren't still inside."

"I don't understand," she said. "After we scared them off, I was certain we'd solved the problem."

"This wasn't done by kids."

"How do you know?"

He didn't have an answer to that, but Gavin knew just the same. Throwing rocks was one thing. Trashing the inside of a house was another.

"It doesn't feel like kids." He ran his hand down the side of her face in a gesture meant to calm. "Don't leave this truck. Whatever happens."

That said, he went back into the house, leaving Tara to wait with tangled nerves for the sheriff.

She was more than a little relieved when the house proved to be empty. Twenty minutes later, she was back in the parlor with Trace Callahan and Gavin.

"It doesn't look like vandalism," Trace said, echoing what Gavin had already told her. "It'd be my guess that someone was looking for something. Did your grandmother keep any valuables in the house, Ms. Delaney? Jewelry, money, stock certificates? Anything like that?"

"The only jewelry my grandmother owned was either costume or made by my father, which, while valuable in its own way, doesn't have any precious stones that could be removed and sold. She kept her money in an old-fashioned passbook savings account, and although I tried to talk her into investing in mutual funds, the only stocks she owned were the floral kind she grew in her garden."

Trace rubbed his jaw as his gaze swept the room again. "It could be a random burglary," he mused. "Except we don't tend to have burglaries in Whiskey River. And then there's the television in the bedroom."

"What about it?"

"It's still there. They didn't take it. Or the VCR."

"Oh." Tara thought about that for a minute. "I wonder . . . No." She shook her head. "That's impossible."

"What?" Trace's gaze was swift and sharp, and suddenly she realized she was no longer looking at the laid-back small-town Western sheriff, but the former big-city cop he'd once been.

"It's nothing." She began twisting her hands together, wishing she'd just kept her mouth shut.

"Why don't you let me be the judge of that?" Trace suggested mildly. Encouragingly.

"It's just that ever since I've moved in, I've thought I heard sounds."

"What kinds of sounds?" Gavin asked quickly before Trace could get the question out.

"Nothing I could put my finger on. Just the usual night sounds. Once I thought someone was trying to get in the window, but it turned out to be the wind blowing a branch against the glass." She'd used a pair of long-handled pruning shears she'd found in the gardening shed to cut the branch away the next morning. "And sometimes, when I'm lying in bed, I think I hear the attic floor creaking overhead. But I'm sure it's just the house settling. Old houses do that," she said, her tone inviting agreement.

"That's probably all it is," Trace said. "But I think I'd better check the attic again, just in case."

"I was up there this afternoon, Sheriff," Tara said. "Everything looked all right."

"Would you have known if something was missing?"

She thought about all those boxes and trunks. "No."

"I'll check one more time just the same." He slanted a look at Gavin. "You stay with Ms. Delaney. This won't take long."

"I feel so foolish," she murmured when she and Gavin were alone again. He'd poured her a glass of brandy and as she sat on the ripped sofa she sipped slowly, feeling the comforting warmth entering her bloodstream.

"For what? Your home was broken into, Tara. And trashed. What the hell do you have to feel foolish about?"

"I sounded like some hysterical female from a made-for-television movie."

"That's ridiculous. And why didn't you tell me you were hearing noises?"

"Because they were nothing." Even as she said it, Tara heard the lack of conviction in her tone and wondered whom she was trying to convince, Gavin or herself.

"I'm afraid I'm going to have to disagree with you on that one," Trace said, returning to the room just in time to hear Tara's statement. "Unless you happen to own a pair of size-ten running shoes."

Her hands tightened around the balloon glass. "I don't understand."

"There are some footprints up there in the dust that look pretty new. Since Gavin and I both wear boots, I'd say you've had yourself some company."

The idea was unthinkable. "Are you saying —"

"I'm saying that either you've got the largest, best-shod mouse in the county living in your attic, or someone thinks you've got something stashed away in this house worth risking a jail term for."

Tara couldn't answer. She merely stared up at him, shock sending a chill all the way through her.

"Well, that settles that," Gavin said, his tone as grim as Trace's expression. "You're spending the night at my place."

It had been a long day, a day of emotional highs and lows. Mentally, physically and emotionally drained, Tara couldn't think of a single reason to argue.

She was grateful when Gavin didn't

speak during the drive to his cabin. She wouldn't have had the energy to answer. As she'd packed an overnight bag, she'd felt as if she were operating on autopilot. She'd been vaguely aware of his carrying her suitcase downstairs, of locking the door — although, as Trace had pointed out, it was probably a bit late for that — of helping her into the truck.

After that, she must have tuned out because the next thing she knew she was standing in Gavin's bedroom.

"You're in luck," he said. "I changed the sheets just this morning."

In the event she might come back with him after dinner, Tara guessed correctly.

"Just let me get some stuff out of the bathroom, and —"

"Why?"

"I figured I'd sleep on the couch." Gavin wished she wouldn't look at him like that. So needy. So vulnerable. It was easier to keep his emotional distance when she was arguing with him. "You've had a rough night, and you're obviously upset, so . . ."

"I don't want you to sleep on the couch."

He stood absolutely still. His eyes narrowed as they swept over her face. "I want you to be very sure what you're saying,

Tara." His voice was low, rough and unmistakably needy. "You've had a shock. I don't want to take advantage of that."

"I've had a shock," she agreed. "But that didn't suddenly make me unable to know my own mind, Gavin." She held out her hands. They were trembling, but only slightly. "I want you to stay with me. I want you to make love with me."

"Sweetheart, I thought you'd never ask." He wrapped his arms around her, drawing her close.

She put her head on his shoulder, drawing from his strength, allowing herself to feel absolutely protected. If this was dependency, Tara thought, it wasn't so bad.

They stood that way for a long time, and Gavin experienced a tenderness wider and deeper than he'd ever felt toward anyone before.

He combed his fingers through her hair, and tilted her head back with the gentlest of tugs.

Tara gazed up at him, her heart shining, unguarded for once, in her eyes. Neither spoke. But in that perfect, magical way shared by lovers since the beginning of time, words were no longer necessary. Thoughts and emotions were exchanged with a stroke of his knuckles up her cheek, the gentle caress of her fingertip along his square jaw, the touch of lips against lips, brushing lightly at first, then clinging as emotions heated and needs rose.

With a deep, heartfelt sigh, Gavin drew her even closer, kissed her more deeply. Although the passion was still there, simmering below the surface, Gavin reined it in.

There would be time for flames, other occasions to ride the whirlwind. Right now it was important that he draw out this perfect moment in time.

As her lips clung to his, Tara lost all track of time. He could have kissed her for moments. Hours. An eternity. She clung to him, drinking in the dark promise of sensual delights to come, and wished that he could continue kissing her endlessly.

She twined her arms around his neck and pressed her body even closer. His heart was pounding; she felt its jackhammer beat in her own pulse. When he murmured something that could have been an endearment or an oath, she tasted his need on her tongue. And when his hands tangled in her hair, then roved down her back and held her hips, pressing her hard against his unyielding hunger, a painful hunger seeped into her bones.

Outside the window, a crescent moon rose in a midnight sky. Inside the bedroom, their passion rose. Gavin's hands, as they roamed over her, creating an enervating warmth from shoulders to thighs, grew more demanding. Tara's arms grew heavy, her head light.

Magic. It crackled around them like the electricity in the air before a thunderstorm; it flowed through them like a river rushing toward the sea; it melted her body like a radiant sun melting hot wax.

Time took on a mystical, dreamlike feel as they undressed each other slowly, drawing out the pleasure. Gavin slipped the pearl buttons of the lace blouse through their silken loops one at a time, slowly, tenderly, as if opening the most precious of presents, allowing his fingers to slide over her skin with the soft strokes of an artist, creating sparks wherever they touched.

"What's this?" he asked, running his fingertip over the silver chain. The necklace seemed familiar; only later would Gavin realize it was the one he'd drawn Brianna wearing.

"It was Brigid's. I found it while I was cleaning. It makes me feel closer to her."

He could feel the vibrations in his fingertips. And although he'd been truly fond of the old lady, it was discomforting to think of making love to Tara while she was wearing something that still possessed so much of her grandmother's energy.

"It's lovely. But I think I'd feel more comfortable, for now, if we took it off."

Understanding completely, Tara nodded her assent. Gavin lifted the thin silver chain over her head and slipped the necklace into a drawer in his bedside table, then returned to undressing her.

It was as if the sun had set inside her, warming Tara from the inside out. Her camisole, a mere wisp of silk and lace, followed the blouse. And then he was cupping her breasts in his hands, heating them with his gaze.

"I knew it," he murmured as his tongue created a hot wet swath across the crests of that aching flesh.

"Knew what?" Her words came out on a little puff of pleasure as his treacherous tongue flicked at a taut nipple.

"That your skin would be as smooth as silk." He treated the other breast to a torture just as sweet, just as prolonged. When his teeth closed around the dampened nipple and tugged, Tara felt a corresponding pull between her legs, an ache that drew a low moan from somewhere deep inside her.

Desperately needing to touch him as he was touching her, she managed, with fingers that had turned damnedly clumsy, to unbutton his denim shirt. "Have I mentioned," she asked in a throaty voice that sounded nothing like her usual cool one, "that your body has been driving me crazy since that first night when I saw you standing beside the fire, your skin gleaming like copper?

"I wanted to touch you. Like this." Her hands splayed over the taut muscle. "I wanted to taste you." She pressed her lips against the flesh that had been tormenting her dreams, the hard dark chest that had glistened with male sweat as he'd chopped wood.

"You should have said something." He sucked in a harsh breath as her mouth heated his skin. "If I'd known you wanted my body so badly, I'd have told you that you could have it."

"Wanting's easy." Her fingers were at his waist, manipulating his belt buckle. "Too easy."

He was about to argue that there had been nothing easy about the way he'd been wanting her, when her tantalizing hand pressed against the placket of his jeans.

There was a time for words and a time for action. And as his flesh swelled painfully against her seductive touch, Gavin decided this was definitely the latter.

They finished undressing each other, then fell onto the bed. His hands were like brands of flames. They touched her everywhere, tangling in her hair, stroking her moist flesh, moving between her legs to discover her hot and wet and wonderfully ready for him.

In turn, she caressed him, reveling in the play of hard muscles beneath dark flesh, exalting in a feminine power like nothing she'd ever known as his stony sex swelled to fill her hand. He was so hot, so hard — his mouth, hands, body. Tara touched, and tasted, and found him magnificent.

After ensuring protection he slid inside her with a silky ease that told her — told him — that they were meant to fit together in this glorious way. Enveloped in her welcoming warmth, Gavin braced himself on his elbows, looked down into her gleaming eyes, then lowered his mouth to hers for a deep, drugging kiss that went on and on and on.

Moving together to a music only they could hear, they performed a beautifully choreographed ballet, their bodies, their minds, their souls, in perfect unison and harmony. The sheets tangled; their hearts entwined.

Tara clung to him with lips, arms, legs. She enveloped him, drew him in, and as he filled all the secret empty places she'd never realized she possessed, as he took her to wild, wonderful places she'd never known existed, Tara felt as if she'd finally come home.

Afterward there was silence. Afraid he'd crush her, Gavin began to pull away, but her arms wrapped around him, holding him tighter.

"Not yet," she murmured.

"Not yet," he agreed. He rolled over onto his side, taking her with him. He kissed her, beginning with her mouth, moving up the side of her face. "What's this?" His fingers gathered up the salty moisture his lips had tasted. "Tears?"

"I'm sorry. It's silly."

Concern struck, driving away the pleasure. "Did I hurt you?"

"No," she assured him with a shaky smile. "In fact, it was just the opposite. I've never felt that way before. It was as if I was flying into the sun. It was terrifying and wonderful all at the same time." She rested her cheek against his moist chest, nestling tightly against him in an unconsciously seductive way that had him growing hard inside her again.

When she lifted her head to look up at him again, her remarkable eyes were glistening with still-unshed tears of pure emotion. "I think it's one of those once-in-a-lifetime experiences you writers refer to as the earth moving."

"I think you might be right." He began to rock against her, slowly at first, letting her feel his renewed desire. "About the earth moving.

"As for the once-in-a-lifetime deal . . ." His lips brushed against hers, his teeth nibbled at her love swollen lips. "I think we can do better than that."

And gloriously, they did. All night long.

12

"Well," Gavin said over breakfast the next morning, "that certainly should have done it."

"Done what?" Tara was sitting opposite him at the table, wearing one of his shirts. The faint purple shadows beneath her eyes gave mute evidence to a mostly sleepless night.

"Gotten the lust out of our system." He couldn't count the number of times they'd made love. He hadn't had powers of recuperation like that even in his horny teenage days. Of course, he considered, he hadn't known a woman like Tara Delaney back then, either.

"You'd certainly think so," Tara agreed with a slow, satisfied smile. She hadn't known it was physically possible for one woman to have that many orgasms in a single night. Sometime, shortly before dawn, she'd stopped counting.

"So want to tell me why I want you again?"

Her mug was on the way to her mouth.

Tara deliberately lowered it to the table and stood. "Beats me. But you're not alone."

She settled herself on his lap. "You do realize, don't you, that this is as much a mistake today as it was last night."

He nuzzled her neck, nibbled at the lobe of her ear. "You're probably right . . . Lord, your skin is so unbelievably soft."

When his tongue made a wet swath down her throat, she felt a jolt of arousal all the way to her bare toes. "It's going to complicate things." She tilted her head back, luxuriating in the way his lips could make her blood hum. "At a time when my life is already unreasonably complicated."

"Don't worry." He grinned, tried to remember the last time sex had made him smile and came up blank. "I'll try to keep this as simple as possible." He trailed his hand up her thigh, stroking her with a feathery touch that brought the blood simmering to the surface.

Tara drew in a deep, shuddering breath as that clever, wicked hand went higher still. "This relationship can't go anywhere," she reminded him as she unfastened a button on his shirt. "When my month is over, I'm going back to my real life in San Francisco. This is just for now. No commitments." Another button followed. Then another. "No strings." She pressed her palms against his bared chest.

"No strings," he agreed.

That little matter clarified, she pressed her lips to his, and together they went racing back into the mists.

Much, much later, after an intimate shower where they proceeded yet again to drive each other crazy, they dressed and tried to decide how to spend the rest of the day. Tara was determined to return to the house, Gavin was equally determined that she not.

"It's dangerous," he insisted. He couldn't figure it out. She was so sweet, so soft, in bed. So why did she have to return to arguing every damn point? She was reminding him more and more of Brigid.

"The house was trashed while we were away," she insisted back.

"But the guy, whoever he is, has obviously been sneaking around in there at night, while you're asleep."

She lifted her chin. "You don't know that."

"And you don't know otherwise." He shoved his hands deep into the pockets of his jeans to keep from shaking her and wondered what his chances would be of keeping her in bed for the next few days until Trace managed to apprehend the perp.

"I can't stay here indefinitely. Brigid's will states quite clearly that I'm to live in the house. For one cycle of the moon."

"She never would have written that damn codicil if she'd even suspected she was putting your life in danger."

Tara knew that he was right. But just because they'd shared the best sex of her life, didn't give him the right to boss her around this way.

"Whoever it was has probably already found what he was looking for," she said, her words sounding unconvincing even to her own ears.

"I'm not going to let you go back there alone, Tara."

"You can't stop me."

"I don't know." He rubbed his chin and gave her a long look, trying to ignore the way the argument had added an appealing hint of pink to her cheeks. "I suppose I could just tie you to my bedposts until the guy's in jail."

The rose flush deepened. "Actually, that's not such a bad idea," she admitted with a laugh. Not wanting to fight after such a glorious night and an even more special morning, she went up on her toes and pressed her smiling lips against his. "Please, Gavin, I want to clean the house up again. I hate thinking of Grandy's things strewn all over like that. And I promised, by coming here to Whiskey River in the first place, to live up to her request."

It was hopeless. As much as he'd tried to fight it, Gavin knew he was hooked. She was crazy, but she was also one helluva kisser. He took hold of her waist and lifted her up for a long, heartfelt kiss that left them both breathless.

"Here's the deal," he said when he lowered her to the floor again. "You can go back to the house. But I'm staying there with you."

A smile bloomed, on her lips and in her eyes. "I think that's a wonderful idea."

They spent the rest of the day cleaning up the house again. Then spent much of the night making love. And although Gavin listened for any indication of an unwelcome visitor, the house, and the night, was quiet.

The following day, while he went to work at the kitchen table on Morganna's latest adventure, Tara went into Brigid's study to continue going through the mail that the intruder had strewn all over the floor.

Most of the envelopes held not only orders but personal letters, as well. Some shared family, work or health problems, hoping Brigid would provide assistance. Others thanked her for previous help and updated her on their progress. All the writers seemed to believe that Brigid would remember them.

Tara suspected, as amazing as it might seem to anyone who hadn't known Brigid, that the letter writers were correct.

Moved by the sincerity of the letters, she sat down at the desk and began to answer each one. She explained that Brigid had passed on, then attempted to address the letter writers' concerns personally.

At first it was difficult discussing — even on paper — such intimate subjects such as adultery, teenage pregnancy and drug addiction. Many other problems seemed to be merely the result of loneliness. In each of these cases, the letter writers seemed to fear a world that was moving too fast for them to keep up. In Brigid, they'd found someone willing to take the time to listen.

The morning flew by. Tara had just realized it was time to leave for town when there was a knock at her door. She opened it to find three women, two Tara guessed to be in their fifties. The other was about her own age.

"Are you Tara Delaney?" One of the older ones stepped forward, a woman in jeans, a sweatshirt bearing the image of a wolf and boots.

"Yes, I am —"

"May we help you?" Gavin, who'd suddenly appeared behind Tara, asked. Tara didn't know whether to be flattered or irritated by his overly protective demeanor.

"I'm Laverne Newsome," the woman said. "And this is Vivien Moore —" she pointed to a slender woman whose sable hair was liberally streaked with gray "— and my daughter, Chloe."

"Hello." Tara smiled at each of the women in turn.

Gavin said nothing.

"We don't want to intrude," Laverne, who seemed to be spokeswoman for the group said, "but we thought we ought to find out what you're going to do about your grandmother's business."

"I'm afraid I don't have any choice but to close it down."

"We worked for Brigid," Laverne said. "Packaging her herbs and getting them mailed out."

Of course. Tara wondered why she

hadn't realized that her grandmother wouldn't have been able to handle the entire business by herself. It was amazing enough she'd taken time to include a letter in so many orders.

"I'm sorry. I should have thought of that, but —"

"We know," Laverne said with a brisk nod of her head. "You've had more on your mind than our jobs. But they were important to us."

"I can understand." It was Tara's turn to nod. "If you'll give me your addresses, I'll have Mr. Reardon send you a check from my grandmother's estate."

"That's not what we're here for," Laverne replied quickly. "Not that we're not real grateful for the offer," she amended. "But what we're really worried about is what all those people are going to do without Brigid's magical herbs."

"I don't believe my grandmother ever referred to them as possessing magical powers," Tara felt obliged to point out.

"You got a point there," Laverne conceded. "But the truth is, those herbs — and the spells she sent out with them — did a heck of a lot of people a lot of good. We think you ought to consider keeping things going."

"I'm afraid that's impossible." Tara felt like the wicked witch of the west when the women exchanged glum glances. "However," she added, "I've spent the morning trying to fill the orders that have been piling up since Brigid's death. If you'd like to help with those —"

"You bet we would." Laverne rubbed her hands together. "Come on, girls, let's get at 'em."

Tara glanced down at her watch. This was her afternoon for tea with Noel. "I was on my way to an appointment —"

"Don't you worry about a thing." Laverne cut her off again. "We know our way around. The orders are in Brigid's study, right?"

"Yes, but —"

"You go on into town," the older woman said, patting Tara on top of the head as if she were a child. "We'll take care of everything."

Tara glanced up at Gavin, who'd yet to say a word.

"Go ahead," he said. "I'll hold down the fort here."

Bemused at how everyone seemed to suddenly be running roughshod over her life, but deciding none of the women looked as if they intended to rob Brigid's house while she was away — and besides, Gavin was here to stop them if they tried — Tara decided to trust them.

"Thank you."

"Thank you," Laverne's petite contemporary said, speaking for the first time since the trio had arrived at her door. "You've no idea how much I've been missing coming to work. After my Joe died in a logging accident, I just went into a terrible depression," she revealed. "I didn't care whether I lived or died. That's when Brigid showed up at my door with a basket of her herbal teas and pointed out that I wasn't the only person in the world who was hurting. She thought that it might make me feel better to help others.

"And she was right. For the first few days, the only reason I dragged myself out of bed to come over here was because I didn't want to let Brigid down. After a week of reading those letters, I realized a lot of people were suffering just like me. After about a month, I realized that somehow, while I was busy working, my melancholy had just magically gone away.

"At first I thought Brigid had put a spell on me. Then I realized that, in her own way, she'd found just the right magic to get me out of my doldrums."

"My grandmother possessed an incredible knowledge of human behavior," Tara agreed, thinking how she'd manipulated things so her own granddaughter would slow down and take stock of her life.

"She also had a kind and generous heart," Chloe tacked on. "I don't know what we're going to do without her. You don't think you might reconsider . . ."

"No. I won't be taking over Brigid's business."

Tara couldn't count the number of times she'd said those words since arriving in Whiskey River. But as she drove down the steep, winding road into town, it crossed her mind that each time she said them, they sounded a little more hollow.

It began to rain. A cold, wind-driven autumn rain that pounded against the windshield, blurring her vision. Reminding herself of the full and busy life waiting for her back in San Francisco, she put the problem away and turned all her attention to getting around all the tight switchbacks without driving off the road.

The Road to Ruin was bright and airy. The moment she entered the gallery, Tara experienced a feeling of welcome that was heightened when a huge yellow dog lifted its head from the floor and began thumping its tail on the gleaming pine planks.

"Tara." Noel rose from behind an old oak desk, her face wreathed in a warm smile. She was dressed in denim leggings, red flat-heeled suede boots and a turquoise fringed top accented with silver conchos. Today's earrings were embossed silver arrowheads. "I'm so pleased you could come."

Moving with a grace that belied the advanced state of her pregnancy, she crossed the room and took both Tara's hands in hers. "You've no idea how pleased I was to hear you'd finally succumbed to Gavin and Thatcher's invitations."

"Invitations?" Tara arched a tawny brow. "Although I didn't read his letters, I have a feeling that Gavin's were more of a summons than an invitation."

Noel laughed. "Knowing Gavin, they probably were. But he was reaching the end of his rope where those kids were concerned." Her smile turned into a slightly concerned frown. "You haven't been having any trouble, have you?"

Tara decided not to ruin her visit by relating the latest vandalism. "Not since I threatened to turn them into lizards and bats."

This drew another laugh. "Oh, I always knew I'd like you. Come into my office. I baked a pumpkin spice cake this morning. And the coffee should be ready."

The small private office was pleasantly cluttered. Two love seats covered in a print reminiscent of a Navajo blanket faced each other in front of a window overlooking a lush garden. The dog followed them in and settled down on a woven rug with a deep, satisfied groan.

The cream walls were covered with family photographs. Tara had no difficulty in picking out Noel's famous sister, the former jet-setting Princess Chantal, and her equally famous brother, Prince Burke, regent of Montacroix. One photo of the prince showed him with a dazzling blond woman who was holding a baby clad in a long white christening gown.

"That's my brother's wife, Sabrina," Noel said, following Tara's gaze. "And their new son, Prince Eduard Leon. But, of course, his name has already been shortened to Eddie."

Tara remembered reading that when it was discovered that the woman he loved could not bear children, thus putting the future of his country in jeopardy, Prince Burke had the Montacroix constitution amended to allow for adoption of the male heir.

"It's obvious that he loves them both very much."

"He adores Sabrina. As for Eddie, it was obvious that from the moment the nurse placed the baby in his arms, Burke considered him his own flesh and blood."

"That's nice." Tara smiled. "Then again, I suppose there are other men who'd feel the same way."

"Ah." Noel nodded and patted her stomach. "I see Gavin's been telling tales."

"He only mentioned that Mac wanted to get married, but you were waiting until your baby was born."

"It's complicated." Noel poured coffee into two mugs. "Would you like sugar or cream?"

"Black's fine. And I'm sorry. I didn't mean to pry."

"Of course you didn't. If you wanted to, you could read my mind and know exactly what I was thinking."

"I was brought up to have better manners," Tara said mildly as she accepted the coffee with a nod of thanks.

"As was I." Noel cut two pieces from the cake that was sitting in the center of the table. "Brigid told me that you were uncomfortable about your abilities."

"It was difficult, growing up," Tara admitted. "Although I was brought up in a nurturing environment, I just wanted to be like all the other kids. Which, of course, I wasn't."

"No." Noel took a sip of coffee, eyeing Tara thoughtfully over the rim of her mug. "You certainly weren't. I suppose, in that respect, I was more fortunate."

"In what way?"

"Being born into Montacroix's royal family already made me different from other children. But I had Burke and Chantal who, being older, helped me over the bumpier spots."

"Do they have your gift?"

"No. I'm the only one in this generation who inherited my grandmother Katia's ability for second sight. Since we were taught that her Gypsy heritage was something to be admired, not embarrassed about, I was never made to feel uncomfortable. However, I have to admit that there are some things I haven't even told my family."

"Everyone's entitled to some privacy," Tara agreed. She took a bite of the spice cake and was not surprised when it was delicious. She suspected whatever the princess chose to do, she'd do very, very well.

"That's true, I suppose."

"Don't you think it's odd," Tara asked suddenly, "that two people with second sight both ended up in the same small town?"

"Actually, I've always believed that there are more people than we think with special talents, people who are unaware of their gifts," Noel responded thoughtfully. "As for ending up here, I've come to think of Whiskey River as a magical place, just waiting for me to find it."

"That's a nice thought," Tara said, not wanting to spoil the mood by confessing how she'd stayed away for that same reason. "I like your gallery," she said instead, seeking to change the subject.

"I like it, too. I've always had an affinity for art — my sister's an artist — but I don't have any talent myself. When I was looking for a new direction for my life, opening a gallery seemed natural.

"One of my favorite pieces of art, by the way, is this bracelet your father made." She held out her arm, revealing the familiar fluid forms of Celtic knots worked with a contemporary twist. Semiprecious dark blue stones had been embedded in the sterling silver.

"Lapis lazuli represents harmony and journeys," Tara said.

To her surprise, Noel burst into delighted laughter. "So Brigid told me when she first saw the bracelet. Who could have guessed that my dear papa would turn out to be so prophetic?"

"You're talking about your move to America," Tara guessed.

"Yes." Laughter continued to dance in Noel's eyes, like sunshine on an Alpine lake. Tara had a feeling that she was about to say more when the bell tied to the gallery door signaled a customer. "I'll try not to take long," Noel promised.

While her hostess was in the other room accompanied by the yellow dog, Tara finished off her cake and drank the rich dark coffee and felt herself relaxing. Though she had no plans to remain in Whiskey River, the idea of sharing occasional afternoon tea with a like-minded woman was more than a little appealing.

When Noel didn't immediately return, Tara picked up a book, entitled *Sandpaintings on the Hogan Floor* from the coffee table. A quick glance at the book jacket revealed the short stories had been written in the late nineteenth century by Wolfe Longwalker, a half Navajo, half

Irish-American writer considered one of the legitimate voices of the American West.

The book, Tara read, had recently been reprinted. She skimmed through the pages and found herself becoming intrigued by the writer's unique voice. Making a mental note to buy a copy of her own before returning to San Francisco, she was about to return the book to the table when the author's photo on the back captured her attention.

Wolfe Longwalker's cheekbones were a sharp slash riding high on his lean dark face; his hair, as black as ebony and as straight as rainwater, hung to his shoulders. His lips were set in a straight, grim line that revealed not an ounce of softness. And although he'd lived a hundred years in the past, although she'd never seen this photograph before, Tara recognized him instantly.

"It can't be," she murmured, shaking her head as she stared down at the book jacket photo. "But somehow . . ."

"Ah," Noel said, choosing that moment to return to the cozy private office, "I see you recognize him, too."

"It's impossible." Tara studied the photo more intently. Although there wasn't any outward physical resemblance between

Wolfe Longwalker and MacKenzie Reardon, she knew the two were the same man.

"Logical minds would say that Wolfe's coming back in the body of a 1990s newspaper man was impossible," Noel agreed mildly. She slipped a small piece of cake to the dog, who was watching her with avid, adoring brown eyes.

"Logical minds would also insist that the idea of a 1990s European princess going back a hundred years in time and falling in love with a man who'd just escaped the gallows was impossible, too."

"Surely you're not saying that you've actually experienced time travel?"

"As impossible as it sounds, I have," Noel said with a calm that suggested they were merely discussing the recipe for her pumpkin spice cake. "My sister had sent me an invitation for a gallery showing of unknown Western artists. The cover was printed from a woodcut entitled 'Massacre at Whiskey River.' "

"Cheerful subject," Tara murmured, shivering at the thought.

"The picture was definitely distressing," Noel agreed. "It was a scene of Indians on horseback watching a settler's cabin burn.

"The minute I touched the invitation, I had a vision of a man on horseback, in the rain, with a noose around his neck."

"And this man was Wolfe Longwalker?"

"Exactly. For some reason I couldn't understand at the time, I was compelled to come here and find out who he was. And why he'd entered my mind." Her expression was thoughtful, her eyes serious. "I stayed at a bed-and-breakfast that in Wolfe's time had been a bordello called the Road to Ruin."

"Catchy name," Tara said. "And now I see why you chose the name for your gallery." She also understood why the princess had laughed about the idea of the blue stone signifying a journey.

"It gets even better." Noel dimpled in a way that made Tara wonder how she could ever have been considered an ice princess. "I bought the house. I'm living in it." Her smile reached her eyes briefly, then she sobered. "To make a long story short, I knew, when I first saw the photographs of Wolfe, that I was meant to clear his name.

"Of course I had no way of knowing at the time that I'd end up in the previous century. Nor did I realize that I was destined to fall in love with him."

"Then you had to leave him behind?" The thought saddened Tara.

"Yes. But miraculously, I managed to bring something back."

Her own family history had exposed Tara to things others might find difficult to accept. But this idea . . .

"Surely you're not suggesting that your child was conceived a century ago?"

"Yes." Noel's hands drifted down to her stomach again in a maternal cradling gesture as old as the ages. "I was worried in the beginning, but Dr. McGraw — that's Nick's wife — assures me that my baby is strong and healthy and developing absolutely normally."

"That's so amazing."

"I know. I suppose it shows the power of love," Noel mused. "That trip changed so much in my life, Tara. And it changed me, too. I was a different person before I met Wolfe. Or, perhaps, it was simply that I'd unconsciously chosen to appear cooler and more subdued because my older sister had already claimed the role of the dazzling Giraudeau daughter. During my time with Wolfe, I discovered feelings I never knew I possessed.

"And not just in bed," she said quickly. "Although that certainly was one of the more exciting aspects of our time together. But I also learned how brave I could be under pressure. And how I could take risks."

"Does Mac know? That it's his child?"

"No." Noel sighed. "He keeps having flashes of memory, but my darling Mac has a very logical nature, so I know he dismisses them. When we first met, it was obvious that we knew each other. But he prefers to believe that he recognized me from my photos."

"I can certainly understand that." Tara considered the position Noel was in, being in love with a man who had no idea he'd fathered their child a hundred years in the past. "This is truly incredible."

"Isn't it?" Noel's eyes danced with laughter. "Even Brigid was impressed."

"Are you going to try to explain it to Mac?"

"If he hasn't remembered by the time the baby's born. But I'm hoping that won't be necessary. There's a Halloween dance at the Grange next Saturday night. I've had a copy of the dress I was wearing when I was with Wolfe made. I'm hoping that will trigger Mac's memory."

"Well, I certainly wish you luck." Tara breathed a soft, slightly envious sigh as she contemplated the idea of a love so strong it could overcome the barrier of time. "Even as complex a problem as this is, you're still a very lucky woman."

Noel smiled as she looked down at Wolfe's photo. "I know."

13

Tara arrived home from the Road to Ruin and found Gavin in the process of preparing dinner. Watching him, she realized she'd made a terrible mistake. He fit into Brigid's kitchen with a comfortable ease that gave her the feeling that, if allowed, he'd take over the house. And her life.

"I take it Laverne, Vivien and Chloe called it a day."

"They filled all the orders that had stacked up." He cut the thick piece of lamb into chucks and sliced and diced the vegetables with the same easy skill he did everything else. "Laverne said she and Chloe would drop them off at the post office on the way home. Apparently, they used to do that for Brigid."

"It's wonderful they could get all that work done so fast."

"Yeah." He pushed the carrots aside and dumped the lamb chunks into the pot where they began sizzling in the heated oil. "Unfortunately, today's mail brought a bunch more."

"I suppose that while I'm here we might as well fill the orders that come."

"Makes sense to me." The oil popped and crackled as he stirred the meat with a long-handled fork. Then he began slicing an onion.

"You're very good at that," Tara murmured, watching the stainless-steel knife flash in the slanting yellow rays of afternoon sun.

"It comes with practice. Sometimes, when I finish work, I'm all wound up. Cooking relaxes me. Clears the mist from my mind."

"Running does that for me."

"I run, too." The onions followed the meat into the copper-bottomed Dutch oven. "But it can't quite compare. Because you don't have anything to eat when you're done."

Tara smiled at that. The smell of the frying meat was making her mouth water. As she watched, he poured some water and wine into the pot and covered it.

"How about sitting out in the garden and having a glass of wine?" he asked. The afternoon had mellowed into a warm Indian summer.

"That sounds wonderful."

"You've done a great job cleaning it up,"

he said, looking out over the weeded beds.

"If you hadn't kept things watered, there wouldn't have been anything left to clean up."

He shrugged. The watering, like replacing the windows, hadn't seemed any big deal. Brigid was a friend. Friends watched out for one another. "Knowing how much Brigid loved her garden, I was thinking about trying to do more, but I figured I'd end up throwing out all the good stuff and keeping the weeds."

"It's not always easy to tell the difference," Tara allowed. "When I was a little girl, I spent summers here. Brigid taught me a lot."

"About more than weeds and herbs," Gavin guessed.

"Yes." Not wanting to talk about her background, not when they were getting along so well, Tara didn't expound.

The leaves on the apple tree were turning gold. Last year Brigid would have harvested the apples to make juice. This year, Gavin explained, he'd allowed a local food bank to take them rather than have them rot on the ground. Soon the leaves would all be gone, leaving the branches bare and forlorn looking throughout the winter. But spring would bring fresh green leaves and white flowers and the promise of renewal.

It was the same life cycle her ancestors had celebrated. Tara sighed, thinking of Brigid, who'd completed the final stage of this cycle, and found herself hoping that her grandmother would someday return. The world needed more generous souls like Brigid Delaney.

"Did you get any work done?" she asked, wanting to turn her thoughts to something less painful.

"Quite a bit, actually. The new story line's coming along great. I'm thinking about having Brianna use her charmed sword to behead the evil gods of Hades who are holding her sister hostage."

"She'd never do that." It was against the character's nature. Since returning to Brigid's Whiskey River home, and meeting Gavin, Tara was discovering exactly how difficult it was to fight nature.

"You know that. And I know that. But I think the reader will buy it. Especially when you see the battle garb I've given her."

"Tell me it isn't black leather." Tara took a sip of wine.

"Nah. Everyone knows Morganna wears black. I was thinking silver, along the lines of a bodysuit spun from moonbeams."

"Why be subtle when you can hit the reader over the head with sex?"

"It's a graphic novel," Gavin reminded her. "The art's every bit as important as the story."

"Apparently even more so," she murmured.

"All her life, Brianna's left the adventures to Morganna. Now she's forced to delve down deep inside herself to discover strengths she never knew she possessed, powers she's never used. It only makes sense that she'd also discover a sexuality she's unconsciously kept repressed all these years. And now that she's aware of her body, she wants to show it off."

His words reminded her of what Noel had said about her adventure changing not only her life but her outlook on life, making her bolder.

"Now you're claiming to be an expert on the female psyche?"

"No man could ever claim that." His hearty laugh was deep and rich. "The female mind is like Africa on all those ancient maps. Uncharted. All you women might as well have Here There Be Dragons tattooed on your pretty, smooth foreheads."

It was Tara's turn to laugh. Then she quickly sobered again. "If I didn't know better," she said, "I'd think you were creating your new plot around me."

"Of course I am." Gavin's easy answer displayed not an iota of guilt.

"Why?"

"Why not? You're beautiful and spirited, Tara. There are times I think you were created from sunlit shadows just to torment me. And how, just when I believe I have a handle on you, you slip back into those shadows and I realize I have no idea who you really are."

His voice was thick. Husky. Tara thought she detected a wee bit of repressed anger in the deep, rough tone. "I'm not that complicated. Oh, I'll admit that I can be a bit stubborn, and —"

"Shut up." His tone was mild, but his eyes were not. "I need to say this." He stood and put his hands on her shoulders, not roughly, but with enough strength to let her know that he wasn't backing off. Not this time. "And you need to hear it."

Tara looked up at him, seeing the man she'd first been drawn to. His dark, untamed looks would send any woman's heart racing.

"You're a gorgeous puzzle wrapped in an

enticing enigma, Tara Delaney. And being a man who's always enjoyed women and puzzles, it wasn't all that surprising to me when I discovered that I couldn't get you out of my mind. That you were always there, night and day, when I was awake, and when I was sleeping. Especially when I was sleeping."

He sighed heavily and ran the back of his hand down the side of her face. "Ah, Tara. The dreams I've been having ever since you arrived in town have been the most erotic and frustrating I've ever had."

"Surely you've dreamt of other women."

"Hell, yes. Like all guys, I've had my share of sexual fantasies. But you're more than a fantasy, more than an obsession. And believe me, sweetheart, I know obsession."

His expression turned grim. His eyes were harder and colder than she'd ever seen them. They reminded her of the piece of obsidian she was wearing around her neck. "Gavin —"

"Later." His tone was brusque and sharp. Realizing how he'd sounded, Gavin cursed softly. "It's time you learned the truth about how I ended up in prison," he said. "But I don't want to spoil dinner with such an unsavory tale. We'll talk later."

He wasn't offering her a choice. But since it was Gavin's story to tell, Tara decided to let him tell it his own way. In his own time.

The dinner was delicious. When Tara began gathering up the dishes, Gavin took the plates from her hands.

"I'll do those."

"But you cooked, so it's only fair —"

"I don't mind. Actually, to tell the truth, I'd like some time alone. To think things through."

Tara realized that it wouldn't be easy to explain to the woman you were sleeping with how you happened to be convicted of murdering a former lover. Wanting to give him the space and time he needed, she said, "I'll be in the study."

"Fine." He managed only a parody of a smile that didn't soften, even after she'd pressed her mouth against his grimly set lips.

After loading the dishwasher and fortifying himself with a stiff drink, Gavin followed the tap, tap, tap of a keyboard into the study.

Tara was hunched over a ledger, her fingers skimming over the calculator keys of a laptop computer.

After returning from her visit with Noel,

she'd changed into a pair of gray leggings and an oversize sweatshirt touting the wonders of a famed San Francisco chocolate company. Her feet were encased in thick gray-and-green striped wool socks. A yellow pencil was stuck haphazardly into her bright hair. She was holding another between her teeth. Every so often she'd stop her rapid calculations, mutter something and make a notation on the ledger. Then her fingers would resume flying over the keys.

Gavin leaned against the doorjamb, enjoying the pleasure of watching her undetected. And as he did so, he tried to come up with a reasonable, logical explanation for his attraction to Tara Delaney.

She was beautiful, but he'd known more than his share of lovely women and had never before suffered such a constant, irresistible pull. Brigid had said Tara was smart as a whip, but so were most of the other women he'd dated. A man who bored easily, Gavin had outgrown gorgeous airheaded bimbos by his twentieth birthday.

The lovemaking they'd shared proved she was a great deal more passionate than the cool accountant image she worked so hard to project to the rest of the world. But passion, Gavin knew all too well, was often fleeting. When he'd first met her, and even more so after he'd kissed her, he'd figured that once they made love, his curiosity would be satisfied, his passion sated.

But now he knew that he'd been fooling himself. Because despite having agreed that their affair would end when her month was up, he was too fascinated with her to be satisfied with a brief, intense fling. He wanted something from her, dammit. And although he still wasn't sure what, Gavin suspected a lifetime would be a good beginning.

As if sensing his thoughts, Tara whirled around.

"I didn't hear you!" Her heart was pounding a million miles a minute. From being startled, she assured herself. It certainly didn't have anything to do with how damn sexy he looked leaning nonchalantly against her doorjamb. *Liar.*

"You looked a million miles away." He crossed the room on a strong stride that reminded her of a cougar stalking its prey, stopped beside the desk and looked down at the ledger sheet. "How's it going?"

"Brigid had many talents," Tara said, leaning back in the chair and stretching out the kinks in her back. "But book-keeping definitely wasn't one of them."

Gavin began massaging the knotted muscles at the base of her neck. "She probably had a lot of company." He vowed never to let Tara see his checkbook register.

"I suppose so. But she was supposed to be running a business."

"Are you saying it was in the red?"

"No." She shook her head, dislodging the pencil. "Actually, she was making an amazing profit. But she certainly couldn't have known it from her record keeping."

Gavin wondered why, if Tara was determined to shut down Brigid's business in order to return to the fast lane in San Francisco, she was spending so much time trying to unravel its financial state. He was tempted to ask, but didn't want to make her feel he'd pushed her into a corner. "We need to talk."

With the gentlest of touches, he lifted her to her feet. "But first I want you." The pad of his thumb strayed over her lips, which parted in response to his sensuous touch. "I want you under me. I want to be inside you." He ran his strong hands down her back, over her hips and pulled her against him so she could feel the full extent of his arousal. "I want to feel you around me, all tight and hot and wet."

The provocative words caused a familiar rush of warm pleasure. "Yes."

He scooped her into his arms and carried her out of the room. Later, Tara would wonder how he'd man aged to make it up all those stairs. But somehow, he did, kissing her all the while, without missing a step.

Their hands tore at clothing, ripping it, scattering it carelessly around the room. Gavin was drunk with her. With the need to touch, to taste, to possess. He craved her with every screeching atom of his being.

He tore away the skimpy blue panties and flung them away before dragging her onto the bed, where they rolled over and over — frantic hands stroking moist, heated flesh, greedy mouths devouring sharp, painful breaths. The animal had burst free of its civilizing restraints; it was dark and dangerous, with jagged teeth and razor-sharp claws. It was relentless.

She trembled as his hands raced over her damp fragrant skin, finding erotic flash points she hadn't even known existed. When his fingers dipped into the warm, moist center of her female body, gathering up the honey flowing there, she dug her fingernails into his back and arched against his touch in a mute plea for more.

"Gavin . . ." She sobbed out his name as she writhed beneath his tormenting touch. "Oh, God. Please." Tara didn't care that she was begging, if that's what it took to satisfy this raw, painful need. She was gasping for breath, every nerve ending in her body threatening to implode as the line between pain and pleasure blurred.

"Not yet." His thumb played with the ultrasensitive nub, drawing a moan from between her parted lips.

Painfully aroused, he watched her, watched the stunned pleasure that turned her eyes to the deep, dark hue of a storm-tossed sea, saw the thrill that burned fever bright on her cheeks as his touch delved deeper, seeking forbidden secrets.

She was wet. And hot. And she was his. Never had he felt such a need to possess a woman. Pamela had been like a mirage on a hot desert highway, always remaining just out of reach. That had never bothered him, since whenever they were together it was as if his head had disengaged, leaving his body to take over.

But sex with Tara was different. Because she was different.

Her body was taut and trembling. When

his tongue dove between her lips he tasted passion. And promise.

"You're mine," he growled, lifting her yet higher off the mattress.

"Yes," she gasped as he pressed his mouth against the heat between her legs. As he began to feast, she cried out, writhing beneath the onslaught of that wicked tongue, that hungry mouth. Her hands flew over her head, her fingers gripped the scrolling on the wrought-iron bed. She was as taut as a bowstring and her breath was coming in harsh, shallow draughts.

"I want you," she gasped as the waves of need swelled. "Now."

"Soon, baby. I promise."

He pressed her hard against his mouth, his teeth scraped against ultrasensitive flesh as his tongue dove deep.

Her climax convulsed her entire body in cataclysmic release and she screamed out his name, not in pain, but in the absolute mindless pleasure of the moment.

His own hunger reaching explosive pro-portions, he surged into her, pumping wildly. And only when he felt her shudder with another release, did he allow himself to empty, heart, soul and seed.

Later, they lay together, arms and legs

entwined, her head on his chest, his chin resting on the top of her head. Her body was still warm, her hair damp. She felt as good in his arms after sex as during, and it crossed Gavin's mind that somehow, when he hadn't been looking, she'd become far more important to him than he'd planned when he'd first decided to take her to bed. Far more important, he feared, than she'd planned.

He took a deep breath, gathering the strength to talk about the worst period of his life. "Contrary to what you've heard, Pamela wasn't exactly married," he said quietly.

Pamela. The dead woman's name conjured up the image of a cool, Alfred Hitchcock blonde in designer suits and very good pearls.

"But she wasn't exactly divorced, either. She was separated from her husband, a billionaire Dallas developer rumored to have mob ties."

Pamela was a mobster's moll? Tara struck the Hitchcock image from her mind and replaced it with a mental picture of the women in every bad thirties gangster movie she'd ever seen.

"He wasn't the stereotypical movie gangster," Gavin said. "He was intelligent, with a degree from Rice in business, and social and political ties in every corner of the state, including, especially, the capital.

"For a time, before his house of cards came tumbling down, both political parties wanted to run him for governor. Pamela told me that one of the reasons she stuck with him, even when he began abusing her, was because she wanted to be First Lady." Gavin sighed. "Like him, she definitely fit the image."

As the peroxide-blond moll wearing too much makeup changed back into the bejeweled socialite, Tara experienced a surge of a sharp, primal emotion she recognized immediately as jealousy.

"Rumors began circulating about some crooked land dealings for property along a planned freeway route. That garnered some attention from the press. As it turned out, it was only the tip of the iceberg, and pretty soon, all the media was piling on. Including me."

"You?" She'd promised herself that she'd remain silent, let him tell his story in his own way, but she was confused by this.

"Before Morganna, before prison, I was a political cartoonist for the *Dallas Morning Herald*. In fact, I'd been syndicated for about six months before it all hit the fan."

"Oh, my God! You're G. D. Thomas?"

The fact that she recognized his name, which meant she also knew his work, bolstered his ego. "That's me. Gavin Dylan Thomas. Gavin for my maternal grandfather, and the Dylan because my dad ran across his books in the prison library. I think the guy was probably the only literary figure Pops was familiar with." Gavin had often thought that the fact that his father had also loved the bottle had given him something in common with the Welsh poet.

"Your cartoons ran in the *San Francisco Chronicle* on Mondays and Fridays. I thought they were wonderful." His pen had been dipped in acid, his wit deadly and right on the mark.

"Thanks." He sighed, thinking back on those days when his career had begun taking off and he'd mistakenly thought he had the entire world in his greedy hands.

"I always wondered why the paper quit carrying them."

"It's a little difficult to find gainful employment in prison. The minute the grand jury indicted me, the syndicate handling my work let me go." The letter from the lawyer had been brief and to the point, referring him to the morals clause in his contract. "The paper was a bit more generous. They kept me on the payroll until the jury verdict came in, even though they didn't run any of my stuff."

"That's horrible. Especially since you were innocent."

"A jury of my peers voted otherwise," he reminded her. "Anyway, to back up, I was enjoying delving into Carrington's questionable business practices, then skewing the guy on the editorial page. The series was nominated for a Pulitzer, which was how I got picked up by the syndicate.

"Then one day, Pamela came by the office with some papers that tied him directly to the mob, and it was only luck, sheer bad luck, that she ended up showing those papers to me. She'd come looking for the columnist who was following the story, but he wasn't going to be around for some time, so she agreed, reluctantly, to see me. She and her husband were separated at the time, and the divorce looked as if it was going to be a long, nasty, drawn-out affair. Carrington was not going to open up the vaults for her, and she was determined to get her share of the wealth she'd married into."

Tara looked up at him. "So she wanted you to help her destroy her husband so she could get his money?"

"That's about it, in a nutshell." Gavin's smile was grim. "It wasn't a bad deal. She'd use me and I'd use her. And in the end, we'd both get what we wanted.

"Pamela was, without a doubt, the most naturally seductive woman I've ever met. She radiated sex like the sun radiates heat. The fact that she was absolutely without morals made her all that more fascinating."

Since she had no idea what to say to that, Tara didn't respond. But she did wonder, if that was the type of woman Gavin was attracted to, what he was doing with her.

"Her husband was like a lot of powerful men," Gavin continued his story. "He had a deep visceral need for absolute control, over everything and everyone around him. It was bad enough to have his wife leave him as soon as his reputation started getting sullied, but to have her flaunting her affair with me — the guy who was publicly goring him on the editorial page every day — was too much to take. So he had her killed."

"And set you up to take the fall." It was not a question. It was also not unlike the plot in all those old gangster movies.

"It was a very clever frame. Especially when it turned out that Pamela was pregnant."

"Pregnant?" Tara's blood chilled. She stared up at him, distress shimmering in her eyes.

"DNA tests proved it wasn't my baby," he assured her, remembering all too well the pain he'd felt thinking there was a chance an unborn child of his had been murdered. "But the prosecutor pointed out that Pamela had told friends — and supposedly me — that it was my child, and suggested that I killed her because I didn't want the responsibility of a child. Since a guy who draws cartoons for a living doesn't conjure up an image of a grown-up in most people's minds, the jury bought it."

"Why would she tell people it was your baby if it wasn't? And whose was it? Her husband's?"

"Not a chance of that. No, tests later proved she'd gotten pregnant by her real lover — the guy who was going to kill her husband for her."

"I really don't understand."

"Neither did I until Trace — who was on the Dallas P.D. at the time, and refused to let the case die a natural death — untangled all the loose ends. He found out she'd been sleeping with Carrington's lawyer, a guy who knew where all the bodies were buried, so to speak."

"He was the one giving her the information she passed on to you."

"Very good, Nancy Drew." Gavin ducked his head and gave her a quick kiss. "The plan was to let everyone, including Carrington, think I was the new guy in her life. Carrington, being a possessive kind of guy, would show up at the house to beat my brains out, and she'd have no choice but to shoot him in self-defense."

"And inherit everything."

"That was the plan. Trace found two one-way tickets to Cancun in the lawyer's office. Unfortunately, Carrington got to *her* first. And since I was the logical suspect, he managed to kill two irritating birds with one stone.

"After the tests proved Pamela's other lover was the father, he told police about their little plan to kill Carrington. He confessed to get off the hook when it came to charges involving her death, and he also admitted that when he'd arrived at the house the night she died, he'd seen Carrington leaving.

"Carrington was brought in for questioning, started ranting and raving about how powerful he was, and how he'd make certain Trace ended up handing out parking tickets for a living, then damned if he didn't have a major coronary right there in the station. He made a deathbed confession, so to speak, and I was out."

"This is the so-called technicality that got you out of prison?" Tara said, incensed at the false rumors that were circulating about him.

"That's it."

"You should say something." She was on her knees now, trembling with pent-up anger and frustration. "You have to let people know what really happened."

Gavin liked the idea that she could get all fired up in his defense. He reached up and ran a hand down her thigh. "What would you have me do? Call a press conference and announce that the good citizens of Whiskey River don't really have a killer living in their midst?"

"That's not such a bad idea," she considered.

"Tara." He could practically see the wheels turning in that gorgeous head. "I was kidding."

"Really, Gavin, it could work. You could

call Mac and tell him exactly what happened. I know Trace would corroborate your story. Then Mac could run the truth in the *Rim Rock Record* and stop all the gossip."

Having had every aspect of his life appear on the front page of all the Texas papers for months, Gavin had come to value his privacy. Enough that he didn't want to reopen old wounds. "The gossip doesn't bother me."

"Well, it bothers me."

He couldn't resist a smile at her indignation. "Why?"

"Why do you think?" she retorted. "Because I care for you, dammit! More than I expected to. More than I should."

Her words mirrored his own thoughts. Gavin held out his arms. "Why don't you come down here and show me how much?" he invited.

Annoyed that he wasn't taking her concerns seriously, that he was using sex to change the subject, Tara muttered a short, unladylike oath. Then she looked down at him. Sprawled on his back, not even attempting to conceal his blatant arousal, surrounded by the lacy pillows and floral embroidered sheets, he looked outrageously masculine and she felt an answering stir of the desire that always seemed so close to the surface whenever he was around.

Laughing in surrender, she fell on top of him and covered his face with a blizzard of kisses, effectively ending the discussion. For now.

14

There were no more indications of any attempted break-ins after Gavin moved into her grandmother's house. And although Trace, who still wasn't comfortable with the simple vandalism theory, hadn't closed the case, Tara was relieved enough to put it out of her mind.

She was also surprised when she realized that she was actually enjoying her days in Whiskey River. Mornings were spent revamping her grandmother's business accounts, and although she tried telling herself that she was only doing the work to keep from getting bored, she secretly admitted it had become more than something to keep occupied.

Although she still intended to return to San Francisco when the month was over, the idea of keeping Brigid's mail-order herb business running seemed more and more attractive, and feasible, with each passing day. Laverne, Vivien and Chloe obviously relished their work; they'd already assured her that they would love to stay on.

She located a gardener who seemed to know almost as much as her grandmother had about herbs, and Thatcher Reardon, bless his heart, had come up with a bookkeeper who promised to take on the daily finances of the business, once Tara got the new system up and running.

Unfortunately, the personal letters to customers would not survive. But this plan, Tara had explained to Noel, over coffee and buttery scones at the Road to Ruin gallery, was better than nothing.

Her personal relationship with Gavin was flourishing, as well. It was as if their physical intimacy moved their relationship to a higher plane and Tara felt as if a dam had burst, freeing a torrent of emotions she'd held back for too many years. She told him everything, about her childhood growing up on the commune, about her eccentric, brilliant father, her serene, yet all-seeing mother, her sense of not fitting in.

"I can understand that," Gavin said. It was two weeks after they'd first made love, and they were in her bed again, lying together beneath the old hand-stitched quilt.

"I think the difference between you and me," he said thoughtfully, "is that when you were trying to find your own place in the world, you turned away from the life your parents had created. While I tried to follow in my pop's not so illustrious footsteps."

Tara stopped admiring the play of muscles across his rib cage and looked up at him. "You wanted to be a bank robber?"

He shrugged, feeling foolish. The only person who knew the story was Trace. And since he suspected Trace shared everything with his wife, Mariah undoubtedly knew, as well.

"Some people might think it's good for a kid to have a goal."

Although his dry tone assured her he was only joking, Tara considered his words seriously for a long, silent moment. "I suppose I can see some logic to that," she decided. "Don't tell me you actually tried to pull off a heist?"

He chuckled at her terminology. "You've been watching too much television."

She laughed and snuggled closer. "Before I met you, I didn't have anything better to do with my nights than work or watch old movies." She lifted her smiling lips to his. "Is this where you tell me I've been making love to Public Enemy Number One?"

"Trying to break into a liquor store

doesn't get you on the FBI's most-wanted list."

"A liquor store?" She stared up at him. "You're kidding."

"I wish I were." He went on to tell her about that fateful night, when he'd had the misfortune to choose a store owned by a couple of cops who'd set up a fail-safe security system.

"I know you probably didn't feel that way at the time," Tara said quietly, "but I think you were lucky."

"You're probably right," he said on a long weary breath. It still pained him, even after all these years. "It definitely put a quick stop to my life of crime. I ended up in juvie jail, just like my dad before he moved on to adult crimes. And adult prison.

"The kicker was that I was locked up when he came home on parole before his last arrest. That time *he* was on the outside and *I* was the one behind the glass window during visiting hours. Let me tell you, it really felt weird."

"It must have been hard on you," she murmured, "growing up that way." Her own life, which had caused her so much distress, had always been filled with love. And protection.

"Life doesn't come with guarantees." Gavin figured they'd strolled down his rocky memory lane enough for one night. "Enough talking," he said as he rolled over and pressed his body against hers. "I want you again."

She gave him a slow, warm smile, then framed his face between her palms and drew his mouth to hers. "Yes."

As Gavin had feared, once was definitely not enough where Tara was concerned. They came together every afternoon like lightning. The hours spent apart — while he worked on his new book in the kitchen and she toiled away on Brigid's business in the study — were an eternity that had to be overcome before they could be together again.

Tara had never known, never imagined, that such passion existed. Occasionally she wondered what she was going to do when the time came to leave the magic of Whiskey River, when she had to give up the sensual pleasures she'd discovered with Gavin. But whenever that depressing thought crept into her thoughts, she stubbornly closed her mind to it.

She had a plan for her life, carefully conceived, thoughtfully mapped out. And as much as she was enjoying this magical time, she tried to convince herself that part of what made it so wonderful was that it wasn't her real life. What she and Gavin had was merely the equivalent to a vacation fling. Their passion, as glorious as it was, could never survive the nitty-gritty of day-to-day routine.

That's what she kept telling herself. The problem was, it was getting harder and harder to believe.

Tara didn't really want to attend Whiskey River's Halloween celebration. However, urged on first by Gavin, then Noel, Laverne, Vivien and Chloe, she surrendered to the inevitable.

"I don't have a costume," she complained to Noel the day of the party.

"Nonsense." Noel waved her words away with a careless flick of the wrist. "Brigid was such a hoarder, I'll bet she has a treasure trove of stuff in her attic. I know we can find something that'll do."

"If I'm going to go through with this, I want something special, like your dress."

Noel had modeled the red satin dance hall girl's dress yesterday. Whether it struck a chord in Mac's memory remained to be seen. In spite of her pregnancy, she'd looked remarkably seductive.

"We'll find something," Noel promised. "In fact —" her gaze became distant "— now that I concentrate, I can see just the thing. It's in a black steamer trunk. Beneath some posters advertising Moira's appearance on the stage of Dublin's Abbey Theatre."

Tara leaned forward, unabashedly intrigued. "What is it?"

Noel's grin was quick and brimming with self-satisfaction and secrets. "You'll see. It'll take your breath away. As for Gavin . . ." She laughed richly with feminine delight. "The poor guy's a goner."

Gavin, who prided himself on his ability to read people, had thought he'd witnessed most aspects of Tara's complex personality. He admired the calculator-slick mind of the accountant, was challenged by her quick wit and frustrated by her tenacity and tendency to argue about what he considered inconsequential things. And he became more enthralled with each passing day with the innate sensuality that was as much a part of her as her breathing. But never had he realized that she truly had the power to bewitch until she came downstairs on Halloween night.

She was dressed in layers of colored silk that at first glance seemed to be transparent, but upon closer observation, only hinted at nudity, while inviting the male mind to create erotic visions that were anything but soothing. Another veil covered the bottom of her face, drawing attention to her eyes, which had been lined with a kohl pencil to accentuate their slanted, feline shape.

She'd smudged more of the smoky shadow at the outer corners of her lids, giving her a foreign, mysterious appearance. Although she wore Brigid's necklace every day beneath her sweaters, tonight she was wearing it on the outside of her costume.

"Well?" With her mouth hidden by that filmy silk, he couldn't see her smile, but he could hear it in her sultry, seductive tone. "Will I do?"

"Do?" The word sounded like the croak of an adolescent boy whose voice was changing. He cleared his throat. "Salome, I presume?"

She held out her arms, which were bedecked in silver slave bracelets, and twirled, making the silk flare out, allowing a glimpse of long, bare leg. "That's a very good guess."

She couldn't have bought anything like that in Whiskey River, Gavin knew. He slammed his mouth shut hard to keep his tongue from hanging out.

"Noel and I found it in an old trunk," she said, confirming his thoughts. "Moira wore it on the stage in a theater where Yeats performed. She was, if the posters were any indication, a hit."

Gavin figured there couldn't have been a man in the audience who wouldn't have spent the entire performance mentally stripping those seven veils off the actress, one at a time, until . . .

"One at a time," she agreed. "Which could make for a very long and interesting night."

"No fair spelunking around in my mind," he complained. He'd almost gotten accustomed to her uncanny ability to read his mind. She'd obviously inherited some psychic ability from her mother, and although she chose not to use her talent, there were times — when she was either nervous or in the throes of passion — when she lost control and did so unconsciously.

"I wasn't." She ran a beringed finger along his jaw before outlining his mouth with a vermilion fingernail. The fact that she never painted those smooth neat nails made tonight's bloodred even more seductive. "Your thoughts are out in the open, Gavin, shimmering around you like a force field."

Like the eroticism surrounding you, he thought.

"I'm so pleased you approve." Her honeyed, satisfied laugh sent heat skimming down his spine, where it wrapped around his body and settled thickly in his groin.

"What man wouldn't?" He drank in the sight of her again and wondered about his chances of convincing her they could have a lot more fun staying home this evening.

"Not on a bet," she answered his unspoken thought. "Everyone, including you, has insisted I show up for this party, so there's no way I'm going to miss it."

"Fine. But we're leaving early."

Tara didn't answer immediately. Her shadowed eyes were making thorough appraisal of his own costume. Although he hadn't gone all out, as she had, the black Western vest, black boots and Stetson, along with the pair of replica pearl-handled Colt .45 Peacemakers in holsters slung low on his hips, gave him the appearance of a very male, very sexy, nineteenth-century gunfighter. She couldn't wait to get her fingers on the snaps of his black Western-cut shirt.

"I think," she said finally, "that's an excellent idea." She reached over and plucked a gold lipstick tube from the table beside the door. "Would you mind keeping this for me?" She held her arms out again. "I don't seem to have any pockets."

"No problem." He gave the shifting layers of silk another longer look. "Am I allowed to ask what, exactly, you're wearing under all those layers?"

"You can ask." Her eyes tantalized, her laugh teased. "But you'll have to wait to find out."

"If I remember my Sunday school lessons, John the Baptist lost his head because of Salome's little dance."

"Don't worry, darling," she drawled, "your head's perfectly safe. I'm interested in an entirely different part of your anatomy."

Gavin opened the door, and with that enticement hanging in the frosty night air, Tara plucked her grandmother's black velvet cape from the coat tree and left the house accompanied by the sound of music.

"I don't recall reading that Salome wore ankle bells."

Tara's answering laugh was as silvery as the bells. "Creative license."

Whiskey River's annual Halloween party looked as if it was going to be a grand success. "I hadn't expected so many people to show up," Tara murmured as she looked at all the cars in the Denim and Diamonds parking lot. "And it's still early." Children were still out trick-or-treating; they'd passed several groups of miniature ghosts, goblins and, of course, witches as they'd driven through town.

"Once the parents get the kids settled down with their loot and a baby-sitter, the place'll probably be packed."

"Tara, Gavin. Glad you guys could make it," Nick McGraw greeted them. He, like most of the men, had opted for cowboy gear. "Let me introduce my wife, Laurel."

"It's nice to meet you," Tara said to the attractive woman who was, amazingly, dressed just like Morganna, Mistress of the Night. "I've heard wonderful things about you. From Noel Giraudeau."

"Noel's one of my favorite patients. With a very intriguing case. Not that all my patients aren't interesting," she added quickly. So quickly that Tara, who knew Noel had shared her time travel adventure with her doctor, suspected Laurel was afraid her remark might have been indiscreet. "I've had so much fun since switching specialties and moving to Whiskey River from Phoenix. As much as I enjoyed sports medicine, after a while sprained ankles and blown knees get a bit routine."

Laurel turned to Gavin, her dark eyes bright with feminine approval. "You are probably the hunkiest gunfighter here. After my husband, of course," she said, flashing a grin up at Nick.

"And you're drop-dead fabulous." Gavin gave her a hug. "If you ever decide to hang up the stethoscope, you could make a living modeling."

"My wife, comic-book model," Nick drawled.

"Graphic novels," Gavin, Tara and Laurel all said in unison.

They shared a laugh, then Tara and Gavin moved on, deeper into the crowd. When she caught a glimpse of Noel, clad in the blatantly sexy, off-the-shoulder red dance hall dress, she started to wave hello. But then she noticed the princess was deep in conversation with Mac Reardon. The look on his face reminded Tara of a man who'd just been struck by lightning.

He's remembered, she thought.

So intent was Tara on watching the

couple, she didn't notice the man in the costume of a sixteenth-century courtier move in front of her. "Good evening, Tara," Reginald McVey greeted her. "Don't you look lovely tonight."

"Thank you." She smiled up at him. "This costume belonged to my great-grandmother."

"So I suspected. It would have been quite daring for her time."

"I think it's daring for any time," Tara said, her smile widening to a full-fledged grin. "You've no idea how much nerve it took for me to wear it out in public."

"That's quite a striking necklace, as well."

"Isn't it?" Tara fingered the obsidian chip. "I found it in Brigid's study while I was cleaning. It makes me feel closer to her somehow."

"I can imagine. I keep her letters for the same reason."

"I've been hoping you'd come visit," she reminded him of his promise to bring Brigid's bowl by the house. "I was thinking you probably know stories about my grandmother I've never heard."

"I'm sorry, my dear, I've definitely been remiss. My travel arrangements have gotten all mixed up and I've spent what seems to be an eternity on the phone with cruise lines and booking agents. But I promise to stop by before I leave."

"Perhaps you can come to dinner," Tara suggested, conveniently forgetting that it was Gavin who did all the cooking.

"I'd be honored," he said.

Thinking what a sweet man he was, Tara smiled at her grandmother's former suitor, then introduced him to Gavin.

"That's quite a costume you've chosen yourself," Tara said. "Surely you didn't find it here in town."

"Oh, no." He ran his hands down the front of his satin coat. "I've had it for some time. It's based on a description of the clothing John Dee wore at court."

He'd said the name as if Tara should have recognized it. She didn't. "John Dee?"

"Astrologer to Queen Elizabeth I. He served her in much the same way Merlin served King Arthur. In fact, he's often referred to as the last royal magician."

"Isn't that interesting," Gavin said. As the band segued into a slow romantic ballad, he turned to Tara. "I believe you promised me the first dance?"

"I seem to recall something about that," Tara said with a smile. She turned back toward Reginald. "It was nice seeing you again. Why don't you call me tomorrow and we'll set a date for dinner."

"I'll do that," he agreed immediately. He turned to Gavin. "It was a pleasure meeting you, Mr. Thomas."

"Yeah," Gavin said. "Nice meeting you, too, McVey."

He led Tara out onto the dance floor, then drew her into his arms. "Weird guy," he muttered.

"I think he's nice. He reminds me of Santa Claus."

"You're kidding."

"Not at all."

Gavin shrugged. "So how come he seemed so nervous around you?"

Surprised by that comment, she tilted her head back and looked up at him. "Did you think so?"

He wondered why, since Tara was supposed to have inherited the Delaney women's second sight, she hadn't realized that right off the bat. "Absolutely."

She thought about that for a minute. "He told me he'd been in love with Brigid for years and years. Apparently he even proposed. Perhaps he just felt uncomfortable about having admitted that to a total stranger."

"That's probably it." Gavin wasn't certain he bought the explanation, but as he could see McVey leaving the party, it seemed foolish to waste time he could be enjoying having Tara in his arms by worrying.

For a while, they swayed to the music, their thoughts focused on later, when they would return to the house and celebrate the holiday in their own private way.

Tara's eyes were closed, her fingers entwined around Gavin's neck. As her thoughts drifted, the vision of a group of children flashed into the front of her mind. They were dressed in typical Halloween costumes, and they were carrying plastic pumpkins. The fact that the pumpkins were filled with candy suggested they were on their way home from a successful evening of trick-or-treating.

Another vision flashed. A truck was speeding down the treacherous winding road leading from the top of the Mogollon Rim into town.

The picture switched back to the children, giggling at the fox terrier who was dancing around them barking for treats, then cut back to the truck's driver, whose expression was one of icy fear.

The children were standing in the middle of the deserted street.

The driver's foot was slamming against the brake pedal, but the truck was not slowing. He cursed, a savage oath ripe with frustration.

"Oh, no!" Tara gasped without thinking.

"Tara?" In contrast to the warm, soft woman Gavin had been holding only a moment before, she'd stiffened like cold steel in his arms

"Gavin," she whispered, "the children!" Drawn by an equally intense feeling of dread, she whipped her gaze across the room and saw Noel staring back at her. It was obvious they were both thinking the same thing. It was also obvious from the terror on Noel's face that she was absolutely helpless to intercede.

No! She couldn't do it, Tara told herself. She wasn't Brigid. Her magic skills were basic, at best. Stopping a runaway truck was beyond her.

But she could not stand by and let those innocent children be killed.

She closed her eyes, struggled to shut out the vision of the children and concentrated on the truck instead. And the road ahead. The grade was steep, guaranteeing that the truck would pick up even more speed.

She considered dropping one of the tall

shaggy green ponderosa pines lining the roadway in front of the truck. But even if she could pull off such a feat, she feared it wouldn't be enough to stop the truck. Or it might cause the truck to crash, which could prove fatal to the driver.

"There's a wetlands around the next curve," a calm voice Tara recognized as Noel's spoke inside her mind. "For migrating birds. If you could somehow . . ."

I'll try, Tara answered, her own gaze skimming across the landscape, until she saw the small bit of marshland Noel was referring to. Conjuring up Gaelic words she didn't even know were in her memory, she implored the help of ancient Celtic gods, goddesses and her grandmother.

"You can do this, Tara, darling," Brigid's familiar voice assured her in loving tones. "You're not alone, darling. I'll help you. We all will."

Tara felt the power flowing through her, warm and golden, then warmer still, like rays of blue heat that got hotter and hotter until every atom in her body was glowing with a white-hot light. She focused all that flaming energy on the truck driver, forcing her inner gaze away from his now-terrified face to his white-knuckled hands gripping the steering wheel.

The truck was approaching the marsh. One more turn. Her nerve endings were crackling like heat lightning on the horizon during a high-country storm.

She bit her lip as she forced the wheel to turn to the right. The air in the cab of the truck was filled with curses as the driver realized he'd lost control. The eighteen wheels sped off the pavement. Mud and water sprayed into the air; ducks took flight with a flurry of flapping wings. The truck sank into the thick, gooey mire with a loud, final, sucking sound.

There was silence.

And then, blessedly, the laughter of children.

Tara felt so drained she would have collapsed to the floor if Gavin hadn't been holding her up. As he lifted her into his arms, the door burst open. "Trace!" an excited male voice called out. "Where's the sheriff?"

"I'm here," a deep voice answered. "What's the matter?"

"I was headed up the hill when I saw a truck veer off the road and into the wetlands."

"Is the driver hurt?" Trace asked, instantly alert.

"Nah, he's okay. But the lucky thing is, if

he hadn't gone into that bog when he did, he would have taken out a bunch of kids who were in the middle of the street around that last corner."

There was a collective intake of breath. Then a buzz of excited conversation. A startling idea reverberated in Gavin's head, but there was no time to think about it. Not when Tara's pale complexion and wide, unseeing eyes reminded him of a wraith.

"I'm taking you home."

Tara didn't answer, couldn't answer. But she held on tight as he led her across the dance floor and out into the crisp Halloween night.

15

At Gavin's insistence, to Tara's embarrassment, Laurel McGraw followed them to the house to examine Tara. After declaring she couldn't find anything wrong, she recommended that Tara come into her office the following day for tests.

"How are you feeling?" Gavin asked when they were alone again.

"Fine," she insisted for the umpteenth time.

"Now that the doctor's gone, want to try telling the truth?" he asked mildly.

She sighed, knowing that she'd been foolish to think she could put anything over on a man who knew all her secrets. Well, almost all of them.

"Other than a crushing headache, I'm fine. I think."

"I didn't say anything earlier, but since you mentioned the children, I figured you must have seen the accident."

"Yes." The pictures ran with horrifying clarity through her mind. "I did."

"Sounds like it was a case of psychic

overload." He sat on the side of the bed and stroked her hair. "No wonder you have a headache. I think you ought to take Laurel up on that suggestion of having some tests done."

"I don't need any tests. I just need an aspirin."

"Coming right up." He left the room. Tara heard him curse. "The bottle in the bathroom is empty," he said when he returned. "If you're sure you'll be all right, I'll run to the store and get more."

"I told you, there's nothing to worry about. And in case you haven't noticed, the nearest store is ten miles away."

"No problem." He bent his head and gave her a brief kiss. "Want me to make you some tea before I go?"

"No, thank you. Except for the little sadist pounding away with a sledgehammer inside my head, I'm fine."

He smiled at that. "Oh, you're a helluva sight better than fine, Tara Delaney." He gave her a longer, deeper kiss, one filled with sensual promise. "You know," he suggested with a friendly leer, "there's more than one cure for a headache."

Despite the pain behind her eyes, Tara smiled. "Why do I think I have an idea what that might be?"

"Because you can read my mind," he said easily. "When I get back, we'll try out a few headache cures. See what works."

One more kiss and then he was gone, leaving her lips tingling in a way that almost took her mind off her blinding headache.

Tara closed her eyes and had drifted off again when the sound of footsteps on the stairs roused her. "Are you back so soon?"

"Actually, I've been waiting for some time."

Her eyes flew open. Reginald McVey was standing in the doorway. "What are you doing here?"

"I've come for the Cortés mirror, Tara."

"What?" She sat up and clutched the sheet to her chin as he entered her bedroom. "What mirror? I don't know what you're talking about."

"This." He reached down and took hold of her necklace. "You've no idea how long I've been searching for it. Rumors have circulated for years that Brigid had the mirror in her possession, but, crafty old witch that she was, she'd never admit a thing."

There was a nasty edge to his voice that chilled Tara's blood. "You don't sound much like a rebuffed suitor now."

"Actually, that little tale was a lie. But it

had a nice ring, didn't it?"

"You lied? Why? And how?" She could read minds, for heaven's sake! Why hadn't she been able to read his?

"To throw you off the track, of course. To make you feel comfortable with me so I could continue looking for the mirror. As for why you didn't know, your powers don't begin to equal mine, Tara Delaney. It was a simple matter to hypnotize you into believing anything I said."

Tara thought about Gavin's unflattering comments regarding the man at the party. "But this isn't a mirror," she observed. "It's only a piece of obsidian."

"Cortés brought back a piece of black obsidian from Mexico that John Dee used as a magic glass. It's currently on display in the British Museum. But there was another mirror, a smaller, more powerful one. Dee's wife, Jane, reportedly wore it around her neck on a silver chain. After she died, it disappeared. People have been searching for it for more than four centuries."

He reached out and his fingers closed around the gleaming piece of jet. "And now I'm the one who found it."

The touch of his fingertips brushing against her flesh sent a surge of lightning through her, scorching her blood while illuminating her mind. She jerked away.

"You killed my grandmother." A vision flooded into her mind, of Brigid standing on the top of the stairs and a man behind her, his arms outstretched. He was furious, his face was scarlet, his eyes bulged; he was shouting obscenities at her.

When Brigid turned her back on him, intending to walk away, he lunged. Tara watched in horror at the sight of her grandmother falling head over heels down the stairs. "My mother was right," she said. "My grandmother was murdered. You pushed her."

"It was an accident." His eyes were hard blue stones, without a glimmer of warmth. "If only she'd just turned the mirror over to me. But no, she was so high and mighty, spouting that old garbage about the right-hand and left-hand paths."

"Brigid only believed in white magic." Tara suddenly understood everything. "You want to use the stone for evil." She leapt out of bed, trying to judge how quickly she could get out the door and down the stairs. He was an old man and he had to be at least thirty pounds overweight. Surely she could outrun him.

"For power," he corrected. "But I never intended for her to be injured. And you won't be, either, if you just hand it over. Now."

He no longer resembled Santa. He was, without question, the most malevolent individual she'd ever met. She also knew that there was no way she was going to willingly hand over something Brigid had died trying to prevent him from getting.

She pushed past him and dashed from the room. Amazingly, given his age and physical condition, he was right behind her as she reached the top of the stairs. His hands reached out, and he managed to grab her shoulders and yank her back toward him.

And then Tara felt a gust of icy wind and suddenly Brigid was back, pulling him away, and the next thing Tara knew he was tumbling headfirst down the stairs, in much the same way her grandmother had done.

He landed sprawled at the bottom of the stairs, grabbed hold of his legs and began screaming curses at her.

Tara was terrified, but the way his legs were bent at ugly, unnatural angles suggested they'd both been fractured. Since it was unlikely he could make his way up the stairs again, she ran back into the bedroom where she picked up the phone and dialed 911.

Then, after locking the door, she sat down on the bed and waited for Trace to arrive.

Gavin arrived at the house right behind Trace. He found Tara, trembling and looking heartwrenchingly vulnerable, and decided that it was a good thing Trace was there to stop him from killing the bastard for trying to hurt Tara. The woman he loved.

Love. It was a word he'd always avoided. Until now. Until Tara.

After the ambulance had taken McVey away, en route to the Payson hospital, Trace took Tara's statement. She told him everything she knew, except the part about her grandmother saving her life. The official story would be that McVey fell while lunging to grab her. Since Trace was obviously a man of reason, a man who insisted on facts, Tara knew he'd never believe that the horrid man had been pushed down the stairs by her grandmother's spirit. She'd been there — she'd seen Brigid with her own eyes — and she hardly believed it herself.

Gavin wanted to call Laurel McGraw, to have her prescribe a tranquilizer. He was frustrated, but not all that surprised when Tara refused.

And finally they were alone once again, sitting in the parlor, in front of the fire.

"Do you have any idea," he murmured, "how much I love you?"

"You don't have to say this, Gavin —"

"Yes, I do." He ran his hand down her face, capturing her chin between his fingers. "I've never said that word to any other woman, Tara. I've used all the euphemisms, but until this moment, I've never told anyone that I loved her. You're the woman I've been dreaming about for years. You're why I invented Morganna —"

"I thought Brianna was supposed to be like me."

"That's what I thought, too — in the beginning, when I first met you. Then I realized that you're both of them all wrapped up in one glorious, sweet, sexy package."

"Gavin, please don't do this . . ."

"I once said in an interview that if I ever met a woman who intrigued and excited me half as much as Morganna did, I'd marry her. The reporter thought I was joking. I wasn't."

He lowered his head until his lips were a breath away from hers. "I want you, Tara. I want to marry you and have babies with you. I want us to spend the rest of our lives here in Whiskey River making magic together."

The idea was so wonderfully appealing. "It sounds wonderful," she admitted. "But what if we aren't the ones making the magic?"

She was so damn stubborn. So sweet. Lured by her slightly parted lips, he covered her mouth with his, giving her a kiss that revealed all the secrets of his heart.

"Tell me that wasn't us," he said when the long kiss finally ended. "Tell me we don't make magic together."

"It's Brigid," she insisted, even as her heart continued to pound wildly in her chest from the aftereffects of the deep kiss.

"Dammit!" Gavin's patience, which had been hanging by a slender thread, snapped. He released her, dragged both his hands through his hair and began to pace. "We've been through this before. Brigid may have brought us together, but it's not like she put some sort of spell on us, Tara. We're adults. With free wills. Capable of making our own choices.

"So if you can't love me, if you don't want to marry me, just say so. But don't you dare try to blame any of this on your grandmother. Because I'm not going to buy it. You need to trust me, Tara, trust what we have together."

"I want to."

"But?"

"But there's something I want you to see, first."

It was important that she get this over and done with now. Once burned, twice shy. And now, before she handed her heart over to Gavin, Tara wanted him to know who — and what — he'd be marrying.

"I'd rather watch you."

The line might not be original, but it made her smile, despite her jangling nerves. "And miss the show?"

Deciding to humor her — she had, after all, had an amazingly stressful night — Gavin followed her outside to the porch.

Tara turned toward a nearby grove of oak trees. The limbs, appearing black in the night light, were bare, the leaves having already fallen to the ground in the age-old circle of nature's death and rebirth.

Breathing deeply, she closed her eyes and cleared her mind. That done, she summoned up the wind, causing the scattered leaves to swirl into a single pile. Encouraged by that small success, she tightened the muscles on her body and began rubbing her palms together, creating a tingling warmth.

As the energy she was raising began to flow through her, she held her hands a few inches apart and visualized it passing from one hand to the other.

Using only the power of her mind and the magic that was her natural birthright, Tara sent that energy swirling in a clockwise direction, faster and faster, in a glowing pulsating ball of red, blue and purple lights. Then she cupped the flashing hot ball in her hands, and when her hands were warm and the energy was at its peak, she pressed it against her body, absorbing it into her system, sending it rushing through her blood.

Opening her eyes, she held out her hand, sending the energy through her arm and out her fingertips. A streak of blue lightning shot across the front yard. An instant later, there was a loud rushing sound and the pile of leaves burst into flames.

"What the hell?" Gavin stared in disbelief at the crackling flames that were shooting upward into the clear black sky. And although he admired her theatrical flare, he wondered how she'd managed the special effects. The quilted robe she'd put on was the key, he decided. She must have rigged it.

"Not hell," she corrected mildly. She untied the robe and held it open, revealing that she had no hidden devices. "Magic."

"It's spontaneous combustion," Gavin insisted. "It happens all the time. In fact, I read not long ago that there was this guy in Winslow who kept a bunch of old newspapers in his garage, and one day they just exploded. Bang." He clapped his hands together. "The place went up like dry tinder. Ended up burning down his house before the fire department could get there."

"For such a highly creative person, you are showing a decided lack of imagination." Tara shook her head. "But you're right about the danger of the fire spreading," she decided as she watched the orange sparks fly upward. She lifted her palm to the clear sky.

Gavin swore ripely as a soft rain began falling directly over the leaves. He was obviously hallucinating.

"Go touch it," Tara suggested. "Feel the cooling moisture on your hand. And tell me it's not real."

Drawn by forces he could not fully understand, Gavin left the porch and walked over to the fire, which was beginning to hiss from the rain. Steam rose and curled around him like a cocoon. He felt the heat, smelled the scent of burning leaves. He put his hand into the circle of rain. The silvery raindrops he captured on his palm. They were not illusions.

Which meant there was only one possible explanation.

"My God." He turned toward her. "You really are a witch."

She nodded, watching his face carefully, waiting for the expected derision. "You don't sound surprised."

Gavin thought about that for a moment. "Strangely enough, I'm not. The thing I *do* find surprising is that I think I knew it all along."

"Well?" She had to ask. "Does it bother you?"

He didn't even have to stop and think about the answer to that question. "Not at all. Actually, I think it's pretty cool."

He walked back over to stand in front of her. "Do you realize how ironic this is," he murmured. "That Morganna, a sexy witch born in my imagination, gave me the freedom to move here to Whiskey River, where I was destined —"

"With a bit of help from my grandmother," Tara interjected.

"With bit of help from your grandmother," he agreed with a slow smile that had her toes curling in her ski socks, "to fall in love with a luscious, real-life witch."

"This isn't how I expected you to respond." Which made sense, Tara decided. Nothing about her visit to Whiskey River had turned out as planned.

"Did you actually believe I'd tuck my tail between my legs and run like that uptight creep you made the mistake of getting engaged to?"

"He was worried about what people would think. How it would affect his career."

"The guy was an idiot. You're lucky you found out he wasn't the kind of man to stick around before you promised to love, honor and cherish. And, needless to say," he tacked on, drawing her into his arms and rubbing soothing circles against her back, "it was his loss."

Tara laughed, because she'd never known that giving her heart to another could make her feel so free.

Gavin touched his lips to hers. "I have something for you." He reached into his pocket, pulled out a gray velvet box and handed it to her.

Tara drew in a quick stunned breath at the sight of the one-of-a-kind ring resting on a bed of white satin. Three stones — a tigereye representing the dawn, silver hematite for the dusk and a heart-shaped piece of obsidian for midnight — had been set in a woven-gold band. "Sky stones?"

"Brigid once told me they hold special significance," Gavin explained carefully, hoping he hadn't made the wrong choice.

"They do." She slipped the ring on her finger and felt a comforting warmth that felt so very right. "They were used by early druids for divination."

"So it's okay? You like it?"

She held the ring up to the streaming silver moonlight, admiring the way the gold gleamed so warmly. "I love it." She lifted her smiling face to his and rewarded him with a long, loving kiss. "I can't imagine a more perfect gift."

It was more than a mere gift. He hoped she understood it represented a pledge. "You are going to marry me, aren't you?"

"Absolutely." Tara refused to be coy. "And make babies with you. Lots and lots of babies. So many we'll have to build an addition on to the house."

"This house?" Although he'd never thought himself a coward, Gavin had been afraid to ask.

"I thought it might be nice," she agreed.

"After all, your cabin, charming as it is, is a little small to raise a family."

"So you are staying." He smiled as he thought about how it was so characteristic of her, with her intrinsic need to plan ahead, to be already creating a new, detailed road map for her life. He couldn't think of anything he'd rather do than travel that road with her. For the rest of their lives.

"I don't see that I have much choice." Her quick grin assured him it was not a decision she'd ever regret. "Brigid, as usual, was right all along. I belong here. And fortunately, as a consultant, I can set up my business anywhere. Although I'll probably have to do a bit more traveling."

"So long as you always come home to me. And all those babies you were talking about us making."

"Always." The thought was so overwhelmingly wonderful, it nearly made her weep. "How about you?" she asked. "How will you feel being married to the Witch of Whiskey River?"

He rubbed his jaw thoughtfully. "It's a little hard to put into words." He scooped her up and carried her back into the house. "Perhaps I'd better just show you."

As a rich, joyous love shimmered through her, Tara laughingly lifted her mouth to Gavin's kiss and surrendered to the magic.

About the Author

Author of over fifty novels, JoAnn Ross wrote her first story — a romance about two star-crossed mallard ducks — when she was just seven years old. She sold her first romance novel in 1982 and now has over eight million copies of her books in print. Her novels have been published in twenty-seven countries, including Japan, Hungary, Czech Republic and Turkey. JoAnn married her high school sweetheart — twice — and makes her home near Phoenix, Arizona.

We hope you have enjoyed this Large Print book. Other Thorndike, Wheeler or Chivers Press Large Print books are available at your library or directly from the publishers.

For more information about current and upcoming titles, please call or write, without obligation, to:

Publisher
Thorndike Press
295 Kennedy Memorial Drive
Waterville, ME   04901
Tel. (800) 223-1244

Or visit our Web site at:
www.gale.com/thorndike
www.gale.com/wheeler

OR

Chivers Large Print
published by BBC Audiobooks Ltd
St James House, The Square
Lower Bristol Road
Bath BA2 3SB
England
Tel. +44(0) 800 136919
email: bbcaudiobooks@bbc.co.uk
www.bbcaudiobooks.co.uk

All our Large Print titles are designed for easy reading, and all our books are made to last.

DATE DUE		
MAR 25 2005		
AUG 2 6 2005		
SEP 1 0 2005		
SF DEC 2005		
FEB 2006		
SC MAR 2006		
FEB 1 4 2008		
SJ SEP 2010		

DATE DUE		
BC MAR 2011		
WC JUN 2012		